"I just want you to be okay."

Piper exhaled. "Why would someone try to hurt me when all I've done is help people?"

He didn't answer and she couldn't blame him. Her question didn't have an answer, not really. But as they sat together in the stillness, she felt like he understood her, like she wasn't alone anymore.

And she also felt more afraid than ever before.

Because he hadn't contradicted anything she'd said. She'd understood his suspicions perfectly, which meant that if Judah was right about why she'd been attacked, she was still in danger. And would continue to be.

Unease crept over her and shivers danced down her arms.

Keep me safe, God, she prayed.

"I don't know, Piper." Judah shook his head. "But I want to find out."

She nodded. Slowly. Met his eyes and felt like maybe they were friends now. Maybe.

"Ready to go inside?"

No, she wasn't, but it was time, and Piper didn't run from trouble. She opened the door. Stepped out.

And immediately fell to her knees as gunfire rained down on them.

Sarah Varland lives in Alaska with her husband, John, their two boys and their dogs. Her passion for books comes from her mom; her love for suspense comes from her dad, who has spent a career in law enforcement. When she's not writing, she's often found dog mushing, hiking, reading, kayaking, drinking coffee or enjoying other Alaskan adventures with her family.

Books by Sarah Varland

Love Inspired Suspense

Treasure Point Secrets
Tundra Threat
Cold Case Witness
Silent Night Shadows
Perilous Homecoming
Mountain Refuge
Alaskan Hideout
Alaskan Ambush
Alaskan Christmas Cold Case
Alaska Secrets
Alaskan Mountain Attack

Visit the Author Profile page at Harlequin.com.

ALASKAN MOUNTAIN ATTACK

SARAH VARLAND

LOVE INSPIRED SUSPENSE
INSPIRATIONAL ROMANCE

LOVE INSPIRED® SUSPENSE
INSPIRATIONAL ROMANCE

ISBN-13: 978-1-335-40527-2

PLEASE RECYCLE
THIS PRODUCT IS RECYCLABLE

Recycling programs
for this product may
not exist in your area.

Alaskan Mountain Attack

This is a work of fiction. Names, characters, places and incidents are either the
product of the author's imagination or are used fictitiously. Any resemblance
to actual persons, living or dead, businesses, companies, events or locales is
entirely coincidental.

This edition published by arrangement with Harlequin Books S.A.

For questions and comments about the quality of this book, please contact us
at CustomerService@Harlequin.com.

Love Inspired
22 Adelaide St. West, 40th Floor
Toronto, Ontario M5H 4E3, Canada
www.Harlequin.com

Printed in U.S.A.

The Lord thy God in the midst of thee is mighty;
he will save, he will rejoice over thee with joy; he will rest
in his love, he will joy over thee with singing.
—*Zephaniah* 3:17

For everyone who encouraged me through the writing of this book. It turns out that 2020 is a hard time to write a book and I am so thankful for every person who helped me be able to tell this story.

ONE

Piper McAdams took a deep breath, did her best to relax against the cold Alaskan rock cliff, centered her weight in her legs. She released her hold with her left arm, shook it out. She was getting worn out—pumped, in climbing lingo—from the route up the rock face. It wasn't the most difficult wall she'd scaled. Maybe a 5.9 rating, she'd guess. But as far as she knew, no one had climbed to the top of it, because access was difficult. That was probably what the man she was here to rescue had been doing, trying to put up a first ascent, be the first one to climb the route and get to name it. He'd wanted to finish it—send it, in climber-speak.

Instead he'd fallen, about fifteen feet from the top of the seventy-foot rock face. It shouldn't have been a major fall, but the rope hadn't caught him. Instead, he'd landed on a ledge below, according to his call to her search and rescue team for help, making his fall distance much shorter.

And Piper was the one who was trying to rescue him. In her search and rescue group, she had the most climbing experience. Also, the rock face towered over

Fourteen-Mile River and just to get there she'd had to use all the white water–navigating skills she possessed. And when it came to swift water rescue, no one in the group was more skilled than she was.

She'd taken their team leader, Jake Stone, with her, to belay her, and Officer Judah Wicks. He and Jake had been having coffee when the call came in, so Jake had brought him along even though this case didn't appear to call for law enforcement presence.

She finished shaking out her left arm, then grabbed the hold again, released her grip on the tiny hold on her right and shook that hand out, too. Her forearms were burning already and she couldn't afford to get so sore she couldn't climb well. She hoped her team wasn't getting nervous watching her. She hadn't understood when she'd first started learning a few years ago that most of a climber's weight was balanced on their legs. You weren't supposed to muscle your way up a wall with sheer upper body strength. Once her climbing partner had told her that, it had been so much easier.

The thought of Judah, her old climbing partner, almost had her slipping off the wall. Piper made herself focus. This wasn't the time for strolling down memory lane or thinking about the one who'd gotten away all those years ago. Even though they still saw each other now and then in town and acted like they'd never met.

Ten more feet to the ledge.

Piper looked down.

Big mistake. She'd managed to corral her fear of heights well enough when she climbed, but the sensation of height mixed with the rushing of the river below her. Her vision blurred for a second, and swirled. She closed her eyes, reminded herself she was on belay and her team leader was holding the other end of the rope. Jake was responsibility personified. She trusted him to secure her well; she didn't need to panic.

Still, coming up here to rescue someone who'd been injured climbing…felt eerie and reminded her a little too well of the ever-present dangers of the sport.

Piper took a deep breath, moved her right foot up the wall to the next foothold she'd identified, and pressed the sole of that shoe against the rock, counting on the friction to help hold her up. She took back her rating for this route. Possibly 5.10. As she reached for another handhold, she thought about climbing tradition and how the person with the first ascent got to name the route. If she made it to the top of this cliff she'd call it Fate Worse Than Death.

Piper took another deep breath and willed herself to stay focused. She concentrated on the cold breeze whipping her ponytail, the sound of the water flowing below her. She felt the roughness of the rock on her hands, the tiny details and texture that made climbing a rock face like this possible. She took a deep breath in. Back out. And finally, *finally*, she reached for the ledge, moved her feet higher and pressed down on the rock to mantle up.

The ledge was empty. The sounds felt different to Piper than they had only minutes before. They were somehow more ominous now, weighty with significance. Where was the climber? Uneasy, she felt a chill go down her spine as she looked around. Someone had made the call, described the place perfectly and insisted they were injured, so… She stood up on the ledge, spun in a slow circle, looking. Then she leaned over the edge, spotted the group at the bottom and shook her head. "No one up here!" she yelled, though she suspected her words would be snatched by the volume of the rushing water.

She started to turn back around, unsure of what to do other than climb to the top of the wall, but as she spun, movement caught her eye, and then she felt someone shove her. Piper felt her legs slip over the ledge and screamed, grasping for her life. Rock scraped her fingertips and she tensed the muscles in her fingers to try to grab hold of something. *Anything*.

Finally, her hands found a large hold, a good grip in the rock, and she caught herself. Pain exploded through her right arm as her body weight landed on it, and Piper cried out as she looked above her. She'd been pushed! Someone had *pushed* her off the ledge.

Her mind scrambled to make sense of what was going on even as she thought she understood. The call had been false. No one was currently in danger except Piper.

She looked down, back up at the ledge. Right? Even if the call was fake, she couldn't risk it; she couldn't leave someone there if there was a possibility they were injured or otherwise in danger. She'd gone into search and rescue work because she knew what having expert help meant to people whose lives were in danger, having been in a situation like that once herself. She cared too much about what she did to give up easily.

Still, there was no reasonable explanation for falling off the ledge like that. She'd been lucky to grab the rock. The last carabiner she'd clipped into was more than ten feet below her, which meant her total fall would have been over twenty feet. A whipper—an intense, swinging fall—like that against a rough rock face such as this one could be just as disastrous as a fall from a greater height.

Piper looked down one more time, then started climbing up. She wasn't willing to live with the possibility that someone had accidentally pushed her, a panicked climber injured from his own fall, maybe. Once again, she used her muscles and finesse to ease her way up the rock, feeling her mind focus in like it always did when she was above the ground like this.

She mantled up onto the outcropping again, this time seeing someone back against the rock face, about six feet away from her. It was a wide ledge, with plenty of room to maneuver. Probably even big enough to camp on.

"Are you okay?" she asked the person, her desire to help someone who needed rescue warring against her sense of self-preservation. This could be the person who'd pushed her…but what if it wasn't and he needed help? Piper didn't know what to think. But she was still surprised when the person came at her in a rush, grabbed her elbow and fought her to the ground.

The figure looked like a man, or at least she thought so. He was wearing a ski mask, so she couldn't see his face, and he outweighed her by well over fifty pounds. His hands went for her neck. Was he trying to kill her? Subdue her? Did it matter?

Piper screamed and fought back with everything she had. And prayed someone below would hear her.

Judah was already halfway up the rock ledge when he heard Piper's sharp cry. Jake had thought he was overreacting, but thankfully for Judah, Jake was only his friend, not his boss. He'd rigged up his self-belay system and started up the rock face as soon as he started to feel uncomfortable, which was when it had looked like she'd shouted something down. There was no reason for her to have done that, when she knew the river would snatch her words away. Her holler told Judah she must be panicked. He'd climbed with her enough in the past to know that Piper didn't easily panic. Something was wrong.

Then she'd fallen. And while Judah didn't know why, he also knew Piper well enough to know there was no way she'd have dropped off that ledge without help. Something wasn't right here.

So he was going up. If he was wrong and she was fine, she wouldn't be happy to see him and he couldn't blame her. The time they'd almost dated and then he'd backed off... Judah had handled that awkwardly and made it impossible for them to stay friends. Since then, he'd been acting like nothing had happened, keeping himself at an even greater distance from her than he normally kept from people.

Which was a pretty big distance anyway. No one had accused Judah of being the most social of men. Or the easiest to get to know. He'd always been someone who preferred to be alone, but it was getting worse the older he got. He'd seen friends...his brother in particular, get hurt, and Judah had figured out a surefire way to avoid that.

Don't have relationships.

He heard another yell, this one muffled, and climbed faster. His heart pumped and his arms were starting to shake. Too fast, he was climbing too fast, and he knew it, could feel it in every muscle, but he didn't have a choice right now. Taking a deep breath, he willed his muscles to calm and they listened well enough that he was able to climb onto the ledge—just in time to see Piper kick at a man, who then grabbed her by both shoulders and shoved her toward the rock wall. She hit it hard, and keeled.

"Freeze!" Judah unholstered his weapon and pointed it at the attacker. "Raven Pass PD. Stop what you're doing."

The man looked at Judah, then grabbed a rope Judah hadn't noticed, up against the rocks, and started climbing.

Judah hesitated. He couldn't shoot a man who was retreating; it wasn't right. And Piper wasn't moving—what if she was hurt? But he hated to let the assailant get away.

"Stop. Police!" he yelled again and followed him up the rope. He glanced down at Piper, but her eyes were closed. She might need attention, but...

He kept climbing, then felt himself hesitate again. The man above gained ground.

But if he didn't go back and help Piper, who would? Jake was left with no one to belay him and, as far as Judah know, didn't have the necessary setup to self-belay.

He was Piper's only possible source of help. And given the fact that she was unconscious...

Judah dropped back down to the ledge, pulled out his phone and called his brother, Levi, a fellow Raven Pass Police Department officer.

"Listen, the short version is I went with the search and rescue team and I think it was a setup. Piper Mc-Adams is unconscious and I need an ambulance. The suspect assaulted her and then fled." He knelt down by Piper, felt for a pulse. Good. Steady.

He felt his shoulders relax. "How're you doing, Judah?" Levi joked. That was Levi, always joking, never taking things seriously.

Accusing Judah of being *too* serious. They were two halves of a coin.

"Levi…"

"Sorry, I get it. I'll call it in. Is Piper going to be okay?"

"I don't know. I need to go."

Levi hung up and Judah pocketed the phone again as he went through the motions of checking on Piper more thoroughly. Heart rate was good. Her breathing was good.

His chest felt tight. Having to check over Piper like this, like she was just anyone when she'd never been *just* anyone to him, was physically painful.

Piper moaned, struggled to sit up.

"Easy, hold on…" He put his hands on her shoulders and tried for a reassuring squeeze, but she fought him. Judah guessed that with all she'd just been through, she might not realize she was safe now. Something else that felt like a stab to his chest. He let go of her, but was careful to keep his hands close so he could catch her if she fell. While she was obviously struggling to regain consciousness, she wasn't there yet…

Another moan. This time she stopped thrashing. Lay there for long enough that he thought she'd gone back under, and then she slowly moved to sit up against the rock wall.

"Where did he go?" she asked.

"The guy who attacked you?"

Her eyes widened a little, like she'd known what had happened but his way of putting it still surprised her. "He got away?"

Judah hated the disappointment he heard in her voice. "I couldn't be in two places at once."

She looked away, nodded slowly, and he felt bad that she understood what he meant. She probably worked harder than half the men in her search and rescue team, proving to herself and everyone else that she could carry more than her own share of the weight. So she must feel frustrated she hadn't been able to stop the fleeing attacker.

Judah shook his head, like it might clear his head. He wasn't much of a people person and wasn't really used to figuring out what others thought. Somehow Piper was different.

He'd suspected that for a while, which was part of the reason he hadn't let things develop between them any more than they had. Right around the time he met her, he'd had a front-row seat to the destruction of his brother's first marriage. He had watched a whole list of other friends go through the same kind of heartbreak. Judah knew himself well enough to know that he was probably difficult to get along with. Used to being alone. Maybe on the gruff side. Better not to get involved with someone like Piper and risk breaking her heart, and his. He'd be terrible at a relationship. She deserved better.

"Hey," he said softly.

She looked at him, blinked. Her gaze seemed clear and coherent. She was beautiful.

He pushed the thoroughly inappropriate-for-the-moment thought away.

"I'm sorry I couldn't get him. And that this happened."

"What did happen?" she asked as she exhaled. "I've been trying to make sense of it, but it seems…"

"Ridiculous?" he asked.

Piper nodded. "Someone lured me up here under the pretense of a rescue…"

"And then tried to kill you," he finished. "You're not deluded. It looks like that's exactly what happened."

"But why?" Frustration was evident in the frown lines around her eyes, the set of her mouth. "I haven't done anything to anyone, haven't seen anything strange…"

Judah shook his head. "I don't know."

"It's been busier than usual for the last few months," she said with a shrug, "I've done more rescues because there have been so many situations like this, where there's some swift water and some rock climbing." Another headshake. "But I don't know who could be upset about lives being saved."

He looked over at her, intended to say something in response, but instead found himself wondering what life would be like right now if he hadn't backed off a year ago. One kiss, that was all they'd shared, but it had been enough to get under his skin, to make him seriously consider what his life would be like if she was still an active part of it. They hadn't dated officially, but they'd spent a lot of time together climbing, hanging out, going out. It had just been about to turn into something official when he put some distance between them.

She blinked. Her blue eyes were clear, the color of a glacial river, so blue they almost seemed to glow. They'd always been such a contrast to her strawberry blond hair.

He cleared his throat. "We've got to get you down," Judah said abruptly. "They could come back."

"But you're here now," she said, like it solved all the world's problems. Her confidence in him was...

Well, intoxicating, frankly.

And just as dangerous. Because he couldn't let himself fall for her. He'd made the choice to be alone in life because he wasn't good at relationships, and at thirty-four, people were starting to believe him when he said he had no plans to get married.

Surely one woman's misplaced confidence in him couldn't shake that.

"I need to get you down," he repeated. "Safely."

She raised an eyebrow. "Five minutes ago this was my rescue and I was calling the shots."

"Yeah, well, now it's my crime scene and *I* am. Life is funny that way. Your rope is still tied?" He looked over at it.

She checked the knots and he nodded. Judah glanced at the connectors on her harness, the buckles, and made sure everything was right. Buddy checks were habit still, even though it had been ages since he'd climbed with anyone.

Maybe he'd been wrong to be so antisocial.

A small part of him was afraid it was too late to change.

"You want to go first?" Judah asked her but they both knew it wasn't really a question. Still, always gracious, Piper nodded. She motioned down to Jake, who nodded and gave her a thumbs-up, confirming that she was on belay in the best way he could since the river was too loud for either of them to hear the other. As they rappelled back down, Judah reminded himself to pay attention to what he was doing, but also found it easy to get lost in thought.

He wasn't a man who was unaware of his faults, despite Levi accusing him of thinking he was perfect. Judah was well aware of his shortcomings.

Did he come across as aloof or arrogant because of the way he held himself apart from everyone else? He didn't mean to.

They both came to the bottom of the rock wall and Judah found himself glancing at Piper.

Was this a second chance at what he'd let pass by the first time? Or rather, run from?

Just as quickly he shook the thought away. She had been attacked and it was his job to investigate it.

His job took priority right now. And if there was anything he was good at, it was prioritizing his job.

Hopefully, that attribute would come in handy to keep Piper safe.

TWO

Piper had hardly been able to think on the boat ride back to town. She'd just sat, listened to the hum of the fan in the boat and let Jake handle the driving. They'd transferred to a police car when they'd reached the shore of the river. Now Piper was in the front passenger seat of the car, next to Judah, who was driving to the police station so she could give a statement. Part of her wished he was more talkative, but he hadn't said anything the whole drive. He just kept his eyes on the road.

Piper replayed the last hour in her mind. She'd been attacked when she thought she was there to rescue someone. Something about that made the experience hurt more, but she'd have to think through it later. Right now, much as her mind wrestled to process it, something in her just refused to.

It hurt. It was wrong.

If Caleb, her former partner, was here, maybe she'd talk to him about it. He'd laugh, tell her to shake it off, but he would listen if she really wanted him to. But after he moved out of town a few months back they'd lost touch, which she'd never thought would happen.

For a while he'd had a crush on her, and she'd wondered if she had feelings for him, but one coffee date had confirmed that they were better off as relaxed friends. There'd been no sparks at all.

And Piper was a girl who wanted sparks. She'd barely dated in high school, focused on the fact that God was preparing a man out there somewhere for her, and acted in faith of that, being careful not to give too much of her heart to a man who wasn't the right one. Besides the one ill-fated date with Caleb, she'd almost dated Judah, and had one long relationship with Drew.

Drew. Now there was a period of her life she'd like to forget. She'd rather never date again than ever end up in a relationship like that again. She'd mistaken his controlling nature for love and it had hurt her. Physically and emotionally.

Now here she was, twenty-nine, and he—her alleged, mysterious future husband—was nowhere in sight. If Judah Wicks was any indication, she chased decent men away with the intimidation factor of a grizzly bear.

She still wasn't sure what she'd done to break up that budding romance. She'd thought… Well, the way he'd kissed her, the way they'd gotten along…

It didn't matter what she'd thought. Reality was what it was.

It didn't help erase the attraction she'd felt for him ever since, though.

Piper sighed, trying not to make eye contact with him. Difficult when she was riding next to him in his squad car. Especially since the attraction she'd always felt for him had never faded, and they were rarely quite this *close* to each other. Eight inches away and they might as well have been touching, for the amount his presence distracted her. It was unnerving for Piper, who was used to being able to ignore men's good looks if she didn't want to pursue a relationship with them.

"You're sure you don't want to go see a doctor first?" Judah asked for what had to be the third or fourth time.

"I'm still fine, Judah."

He glanced back at her anyway and she felt her cheeks heat. Probably the way she said his name conveyed more emotion than she meant for it to. It wasn't her fault she'd wondered all year what she'd done to destroy her chances with him.

It wasn't that he was such a catch, objectively. Well, he was, but he wasn't perfect. Piper could see his flaws, but he was so…determined. Committed. Good at his job and not showy about it.

He was the epitome of the strong, silent type, tall dark and handsome, and whatever other romantic clichés were lurking about in her mind. For some reason, they all reminded her of Judah. And he…

Was not interested in her. And had made that perfectly clear.

If only she knew what made him draw away… Was she not good enough? Judah had never said that last part—her own mind had filled it in—but it was possible.

Judah seemed to have more on his mind than just the trip to the station, and was probably already thinking through the case, trying to work out the whos, the whys, all of it.

She liked that he'd been the one to climb up after

her. She'd known when she saw him that she would be okay. His presence did that to her.

God, should I feel so strongly for someone who doesn't even want friendship from me? He wants no relationship at all, Lord, and it would be so easy for me to fall for him even more than I have. Help me?

"Piper, please? Just a quick checkup. It will make me feel better."

She looked at him and sighed, but finally nodded. "We can go now. There's a doctor at the clinic who has told us to call if we're hurt in a rescue and she'll see us right away."

He drove her there and offered to come inside, but she told him to wait in the car. The doctor gave her a checkup and decided nothing was damaged enough to warrant further attention. Piper would just have some bruises.

She made her way back out of the office to Judah's waiting car, ready with more questions for him.

He had one for her first. "What did the doctor say?"

"She said I'm fine. I told you I didn't need to come in." She didn't know why she was being snappy with him, except that it was strange that he cared so much. Maybe that had her off balance—that and the unexpected events of earlier. Piper took a deep breath, made her best attempt at a peace offering. "She did say it was good I came in, so thank you." She gave a small smile, which Judah returned.

Now, for her questions. "So, besides my report, why else did you want me to come down?"

"Why else?" He repeated her question. If that was his version of clueless, he wasn't very good at it. She made a mental note that for all his standoffishness, Judah was not good at evading the truth. She had a feeling he'd never lied in his life.

She appreciated that. But it was funny to see him try to avoid answering a question while not violating his personal ethics.

"You know what I'm asking. You've been lost in thought since we started to rappel and I'm guessing you've already got a plan for solving this."

He shook his head. "You give me too much credit, Piper."

"So you're really driving me there to get my official statement and that's all?"

He hesitated and she wished she knew what he was thinking. Unfortunately for her, Judah hid his thoughts and feelings too well, and no evidence of them showed on his face or in his eyes. She'd always noticed the way his dark eyes gave away nothing of his feelings. They were nice eyes, though, handsome like the rest of him. Judah was every bit the poster child for a clean-cut, handsome law enforcement officer, down to the freshly shaven, well-chiseled jawline, and the dimple on his cheek when he smiled.

Which he wasn't doing right now. He looked serious. Too serious.

"I'd like to talk about your last few rescues."

Not what she'd been expecting to hear. "My what?"

"You said earlier, on the rock," he continued, his voice even, "that you didn't know who could get upset about lives being saved. I kept thinking about that as we rappelled. You know who could get upset about that?

People who meant to kill someone. Maybe they were in the middle of a murder and it was interrupted."

Piper blinked. Blinked again.

"Wait, what? You think someone tried to kill someone and I stopped them?"

"Possibly. It would provide a reason for them to want you out of the way."

She considered it. It wasn't absurd, but it was still difficult to wrap her mind around. Search and rescue was a good job; it involved helping people. Piper knew her work was dangerous and had counted that cost and deemed it acceptable. But she'd never reckoned on this kind of danger. It rubbed her wrong.

"You okay?"

She thought again about how much the attack had bothered her, and not just because of fear. She didn't have anyone else to talk to, but maybe…

Could she talk to Judah? Ignore her silly crush or whatever it was and just treat him as a friend?

"I'm not sure if I am."

She felt him hit the brake immediately. "Should we go back to the doctor?"

"Judah. I'm physically fine. Today is just messing with my mind, that's all." Had he been asking how she was mentally or had he only been concerned about whether or not she was hurt? Piper stared out the window, second-guessing her decision to try to talk to him. No need to force a bond that wasn't there, right? She had other people she could talk to.

Except, who? Her old friends were busy with their own lives. Like there was something in the air, the other people in her SAR team were falling in love one by one.

First Jake, when his first love, Cassie, had returned to town. Then Adriana had found Levi, Judah's more light-hearted brother. And then Ellie, whom Piper had never expected to be so head over heels for anyone.

They were all still friends and they'd listen if Piper needed them to, she knew that. But she didn't like to bother them when they were involved in their own lives now.

"The attack?"

Piper nodded, still looking out the window. They drove in silence to the police station and she tried to ignore the hurt that he didn't ask more, didn't encourage her to talk. It wasn't his job; he didn't have to. He owed her nothing. No matter how much she repeated those truths to herself, though, she still felt alone.

They pulled into the lot and Piper reached for the door handle. Before she had a chance to open it, Judah's voice stopped her.

"What bothers you most about it?"

She stopped. The casual tone was perfect. No pressure. The question itself didn't assume he knew how she felt, but also acknowledged that it might be complicated.

"I…" She trailed off. "You sure you don't mind talking about this?" She shifted in her seat to face him, taking in the breadth of his shoulders, his sharp jawline. His face was tense, and she knew he, too, was still calming down from the experience. Was he really okay talking through it with her?

"I don't mind. I just want you to be okay."

Piper exhaled. "Why would someone try to hurt me when all I've done is help people?"

He didn't answer and she couldn't blame him. Her

question didn't have an answer, not really. But as they sat together in the stillness, she felt like he understood her, like she wasn't alone anymore.

And she also felt more afraid than ever before.

Because he hadn't contradicted anything she'd said. She'd understood his suspicions perfectly, which meant that if Judah was right about why she'd been attacked, she was still in danger. And would continue to be.

Unease crept over her and shivers danced down her arms.

Keep me safe, God, she prayed.

"I don't know, Piper." Judah shook his head. "But I want to find out."

She nodded. Slowly. Met his eyes and felt like maybe they were friends now. Maybe.

"Ready to go inside?"

No, she wasn't, but it was time, and Piper didn't run from trouble. She nodded slowly and opened the door. Stepped out.

And immediately fell to her knees as gunfire rained down on them.

Judah couldn't get to Piper fast enough. At the pop-pop-pop of gunshots, he dove to the dirt and crawled to the other side of the car. The dust was flying, getting in his mouth and making him taste dirt and fear. Those shots had been too close, not quite hitting the car, but almost. When he reached her, Piper had already ducked and curled into a ball.

"You okay?" he asked, heart still pounding. It was one thing to be fairly certain someone was after her. It was another to have gunfire involved.

Someone wanted Piper out of the picture. Immediately. The thought turned Judah's insides to solid ice. It terrified him more than anything had in a long time.

She shook her head, finally answering his question.

His breath caught. "You're hit?"

"No." She said around a shuddery breath. "I'm not hit. Sorry. I'm just not fine. Someone's shooting at us—you know that, right?"

Judah was pretty sure they were shooting specifically at her, but guessed that wouldn't go very far to making her feel better. So he kept his mouth shut.

The gunfire, which had stopped for the span of two or three seconds, started up again. Judah pulled Piper closer to him, feeling unexpected butterflies in his stomach at her nearness. That was something that never happened when he was working, and he was used to protecting people. Was he really still hung up on Piper from all those months ago? Judah didn't know; right now it didn't matter. Protecting her mattered. There was nowhere to go. The route from the car to the police station door was unprotected and there was no way either one of them could outrun a bullet. In extreme situations where people had to run, Judah knew that a zigzag pattern was preferable, but sheltering in place behind a car was even more so.

"Hang on. Someone inside will hear. It can't last long." He hated the feeling of vulnerability, of not being able to help, but there was little he could do. The shots were coming from the driver's side of the car, somewhere in the woods, but he couldn't just stand up and start shooting, like people did in the movies. That wasn't how life worked—a good marksman never shot without being sure of his target. And right now there was no target, only the echo of silence.

The shots had stopped.

Judah could hear Piper breathing, could feel her body tremble slightly under his arms. He was still pressed up against her, and finally realized his arms were still wrapped around her and probably...didn't...need to be.

"Sorry," he mumbled as he released his hold.

"Don't." She pulled him back to her and took a deep, long breath. The trembling lessened. He waited. Finally, she scooted away and he dropped his arms.

"Thank you," she said calmly, not seeming in the least embarrassed of her fear. Some women would have been mortified. Some would have been overly confident. Piper admitted she was afraid and wasn't ashamed of it. She didn't let it control her, but wasn't sorry, either.

There was something beautiful in that. Maybe that was why she was the one woman he'd never been able to forget. Because, to her core, Piper was unforgettable.

"How are we going to get inside?" she asked just as the double doors in front of the building opened. Several officers ran out, guns drawn but pointed at the ground.

"Wicks, you see anything?" Officer Cook asked as he hurried toward them.

"No, but shots came from that way." He pointed. The officers dispersed, searching the scene. They came back moments later, shaking their heads. They hadn't found anyone. Judah stood, then reached down to help Piper to her feet.

Her dark blue eyes were serious, somber.

"I still don't understand why saving lives would be dangerous in this way." She shrugged. "I know it probably sounds ridiculous to someone who risks his life regularly, but this isn't what I signed up for. I don't want to be under this kind of threat."

Judah nodded. "I understand."

"You can look into my old cases if you want, but for now, could I give my statement and then go home?"

"I don't see anything," Officer Cook said. "Get her inside."

Judah grabbed Piper's hand and took her with him into the building. No shots erupted; nothing appeared wrong at all. There was the slightest breeze through the trees, but besides that, everything was fairly still.

Eerily so. He couldn't blame her for wanting to go home, though part of him was...

What, disappointed? Who got disappointed that a woman who'd been through the kind of trauma she had been in the last few hours didn't want to subject herself to more? He shouldn't have assumed she'd want to be involved in trying to figure out who was after her. And definitely shouldn't have assumed that she'd be okay with the visit to the station just because he would be there with her. They were friends maybe, barely. But she'd been through a lot.

"Yes," he said as they went through the front doors. "I'll take you home right after this."

"My car is at the search and rescue headquarters," she reminded him.

"I'll drive you there and then follow you home."

She opened her mouth. To argue about his wanting to follow her? But then she closed it.

"The room where we can talk is this way." He led

her inside and told her to sit down. "All right, so tell me what happened when you climbed the rock."

Piper walked him through the story and he took notes, crafting the official report. Paperwork wasn't his favorite part of the job, but while he knew some officers who rushed through it, Judah believed it was best to do it right the first time and get as many details as possible.

"So, when you first topped out on that ledge, did you see the person?" he asked her.

"No." Piper shook her head. "That's when I leaned back down and yelled to you guys."

"We couldn't hear over the river."

"I wondered about that." She nodded. Her facial expression was more neutral now and it seemed she had regained some of her composure.

"Go on," he requested.

"I turned back to the ledge and a man came toward me," she continued, and Judah felt his fists clenching. The idea that a man would attack a woman at all was repulsive, but that the target was *this* woman made it hurt more. Added to that was the fact that rock climbing was inherently dangerous, but it was a type of calculated risk. Whoever had done this had obliterated the ability to calculate those risks. It was another aspect that would be frustrating to Piper, he knew.

As she detailed the rest of the attack, including the vague details she'd managed to remember of her assailant—probably a man, large—he had to remind himself to breathe deeply, and that she was safe now.

But as they finished up and she asked if she could leave, he realized that was part of the problem.

She wasn't safe now.

And leaving wasn't going to make her any safer. Judah wanted to stop her, tell her that assisting him with the case could make it go faster, but he guessed it probably wouldn't help. She seemed set in her decision, and Piper had never seemed to him like a woman who changed her mind easily. She knew what she wanted and she did it. If she wanted out of the investigative side of things, she could be.

Judah just hoped they could get enough information about her searches without her assistance, to piece together why someone would be after her. Because they'd need to find that out in order to remove the threat against her.

Her leaving made his job harder, but Judah was determined to do it well. And quickly. Then Piper would be back out of his life. He'd have no reason to get distracted by her all-too-compelling eyes, and could go back to his normal, predictable life.

That was what he wanted…right?

THREE

Judah and Piper got back into the police car and headed for search and rescue headquarters. Her car was back there and Judah had promised to take her.

"You want to talk about today at all anymore?" Judah asked. He didn't usually like to talk things out, but Piper might, so it felt kind to offer.

"No." Her voice was short. "I don't. I want to forget it happened and go on with my life."

That wasn't an option, but maybe now wasn't the time to make sure she knew that. Trouble had already come to her, and much as she might prefer to bury her head in the sand, the only thing to do was face the trouble. Stare it down and beat it.

"You're handling it better than you think you are," he finally said.

She looked at him and met his gaze. He forced himself not to break eye contact and she nodded once. "Thank you."

His shoulders relaxed as she looked away. He hadn't realized he was tense, but Piper affected him, all of his emotions.

"We're here," he commented as they pulled in, though their location was obvious and probably he was just talking to fill the space.

"Thanks for the ride," she said, her voice friendly.

"You're welcome. I'll follow you home and check your house."

"There's really no need for you to do that."

"Piper, I am not asking you." He finally put a little more firmness in his voice. "And it's not…you know… It's something we would do for anyone. Police protocol in a situation like this to keep you safe."

She nodded. "Fine."

Judah followed her home; then he walked through her house and cleared the rooms one by one. No one was inside.

The house itself wasn't a surprise at all. The inside was airy and light, lots of white but also lots of random pieces that were bright colors. It was a fun, quirky look that suited Piper.

"Thanks for checking on everything. I shouldn't have fought you on that," Piper started. "It's not you, it's just the day. I'm overwhelmed, I think, and it's not really helping my attitude much."

He nodded. "Thanks, Piper." He hesitated, debating saying anything else, and then decided it was time to leave. "Make sure you call me if there's any hint of trouble," he said as he climbed into his car.

She nodded. "I will. I promise."

Judah sat there in the car for another minute, not quite ready to go. If he left now, would they go back to how it had been after they'd sort-of-dated? Where he worked with her now and then but there was just an overwhelming awkwardness and a giant question mark about what might have been hanging over his head?

Besides that, there was her safety to consider. If he left now and anything happened, he would never forgive himself. And it wasn't outside the realm of possibility. She'd been attacked twice within a matter of a few hours. Piper sighed audibly and came up to his car window.

"Are you leaving? I've got to head inside." She smiled apologetically. "I'm sorry, Judah, but I'm exhausted. It's been an awful day, and to be honest, I'd love to have some coffee and take a shower. If you want to talk more, can we do that later?"

"Sorry." He cleared his throat. What was wrong with him? This wasn't him, bumbling and overprotective. With anyone else, he'd have checked the house, told them it was fine and left.

Why did Piper have to be the one who was attacked?

"Have a good night," he told her as he put the car in Reverse.

She nodded, smiled in his direction and waved as he started to pull out. So at least he was fairly sure he hadn't offended her.

He was halfway out of the driveway when his phone rang. Piper had already closed the door and gone inside. Judah pressed the brake, put the car in Drive again and pulled forward. It was easier to talk when he wasn't driving. He glanced at the phone. It was Levi. "Hello?" He put the car back in Park.

"Judah, you okay, man?"

"I'm fine."

"I just got into work and heard about the rest of your

day. Maybe you could let your brother know when you narrowly escape death multiple times in a shift?"

Judah frowned. He'd wished more than once his brother would be less flippant about things.

"I'm fine," he repeated instead.

"Seriously, Judah." Levi's voice was even, calm. Not like his brother at all. Judah felt his shoulders relax. Maybe Levi was capable of being more thoughtful and earnest. He had to admit he'd been impressed by the way Levi had handled the danger the woman he loved had been in. It was time to let his little brother be who he was.

Maybe it was time for Judah to figure out who *he* was.

"Really, I'm okay. I'm sitting in front of Piper Mc-Adams's house right now."

"She's all right?"

"Physically. Mentally she's pretty shaken up." He kept looking at the house, watched as one light came on and then another, as she walked through the rooms. The shades were closed, so he couldn't see her, but he still felt a little too much like a stalker for comfort. He looked away.

"Levi?"

"Yeah?"

"I don't want to leave her here alone." He spoke the words and then left them there, with no more explanation. Probably more wasn't needed, but even if it was, Judah didn't know what to say. All he knew was that now that he'd had time to think about it, he wasn't comfortable with it. Department protocol said she was fine. The department didn't have manpower to put protective details on people, just to respond to and investigate crime. But Judah's shift ended in just a few minutes.

"So don't."

"It's not that easy." Judah ran a hand through his hair. Then again, why wasn't it that easy? He could stay.

But should he?

"Judah?" Levi said his name and waited. Judah looked back up at the house.

"Yeah?" he asked his brother.

"It's okay to care about somebody."

Judah disagreed. He had no plans to care about her more than he did any other human. But he didn't want her to get hurt.

He leaned his seat back. "Don't get all sappy." He told his brother. "Nothing's going on between us." He felt a little twinge at the unintentional lie of omission. Something *had* gone on between them a year ago and Levi didn't know that. But it was true that nothing was now.

"Sure."

"I just want her to stay alive."

Piper had known she wouldn't sleep well, but she'd thought she'd sleep some. Instead she found herself tossing and turning, replaying the fall in her head, wondering how close she'd come to dying, and if she could have done anything differently.

She should have stuck around the police department longer, talked Judah through all her recent cases. Or they could have gotten copies of the records from Raven Pass SAR headquarters, and she could have looked through them with him.

Maybe then she'd have had someone to talk to, to process with. But she'd been too…scared? Uncertain? Embarrassed by her attraction to Judah, which she wasn't sure she could hide?

The truth was, when he'd taken her in his arms to protect her earlier, she'd had the oddest feeling that he was what she'd been waiting for, her entire life. *Whom* she'd been waiting for. It wasn't love at first sight. She'd seen him before, kissed him. Climbed with him. But still, today had been out of the ordinary, and the amount of attraction she'd felt toward Judah was part of that.

Why did he affect her so much?

It was partly because of that that Piper had decided to come home. But truthfully, she'd also felt she was in the way at the police department. Piper was good at search and rescue, but she knew nothing about investigating. Judah had asked her to help, but it seemed like he just wanted to keep her close. Judah always wanted to protect people he knew—and even those he didn't. That was why he was such a good officer.

The main problem, she decided, and the legitimate reason she'd come home, was that she was a liability to Judah and she knew it. Why offer to help when he had it under control and didn't need her? What if she was there pretending to be useful and she only distracted him?

Piper didn't know. She was getting a headache. She rolled over again, closed her eyes tighter as though that would help sleep come.

Of all the people who could have climbed up the rock after her, why Judah? She'd asked God that question more than once today and had gotten no answer. Judah was one of the last people on earth she'd voluntarily be vulnerable around; after all, she did tend to learn her lesson after making a mistake, and trying to date him had most definitely been that. But he had been the one who was there. And Piper didn't believe in accidents.

What are You up to here, God? she asked as she rolled over again. No answer. God heard her; she knew that. But it would be nice if she received immediate answers every time she spoke to Him.

Finally she gave up on sleep, at least for now. She started down the stairs, then stopped as something outside caught her eye. There was a vehicle in her driveway. She blinked the nighttime dryness away.

Judah's patrol car.

Had something happened right as he was about to leave? But that was hours ago. She ran down the rest of the stairs. Surely he'd left, right? Piper tried to remember if she'd looked out the window since then but couldn't.

He hadn't stayed...

Had he?

Piper eased her front door open. Started toward the car.

"What are you doing?" A low voice behind her made her jump. Judah.

She whirled around. "What are *you* doing, sneaking up on people like that?"

He laughed softly. "I didn't mean to scare you." He reached for her arm, moved her back toward the house. "You need to get back inside, though."

"And you need to go home," she said as she let him guide her toward the front door.

"Piper." His voice was serious now.

"Have you been in the car all night?" she asked as she stepped inside. He stood on the front porch.

"Yes. And I'm staying there until morning. I was out because I heard something I needed to check out."

The midnight moment was over. Piper was back to earth now, fully remembering all the danger she had faced earlier, feeling like she was right back there, falling off that rock face again.

"I was fine being here alone," she said, though she wondered if it were true. If she were fine, would he have stayed? The answer seemed obvious.

"You were. Now go inside and we'll talk about it tomorrow."

"Come inside and talk to me for a while?" she asked. "I can't sleep."

He hesitated. Then nodded. "For a few minutes."

Piper moved aside so he could come into the house, and locked the door behind him. "Do you want a cup of coffee?" She felt her heartbeat quicken. There was something unusual about having a man inside her house at all, much less in the middle of the night. But her invitation hadn't been meant in any kind of inappropriate way. She just…she almost felt like she'd run away after visiting the police department. Sure, it had been done calmly, but rather than get involved she'd asked to leave, had tried to hide away in her house and pretend like everything was all right.

Even if she couldn't quite figure out if she had been hiding from danger or from Judah. Or maybe both.

The fact that she couldn't sleep was enough evidence that she didn't really believe that lie she had attempted to tell herself. Everything was certainly *not* okay.

"I'd take a cup."

His eyes were tired, and she noticed for the first time the way they crinkled in the corner a little. Laugh lines? She wouldn't have said Judah Wicks spent much time laughing.

No, she corrected herself immediately as she moved to make the coffee. She went through the motions of grinding the beans, adding them to the filter basket. The Judah she'd first met a year ago had laughed plenty. He wasn't like this.

What had happened to change him?

Judah knew that Levi would call him out if he were here right now. Sitting in someone's driveway because you were worried about their physical safety was one thing. Going into the living room and having coffee with them because you could tell they needed to talk and you were worried about their mental well-being was another thing entirely.

Piper seemed okay. Better than she had earlier in the evening, in fact, even though Judah guessed she hadn't slept well. He wasn't sure what to ask her, though, didn't quite know how to talk to her.

Maybe coffee had been a mistake. He felt pressure in his throat as he realized that even if she did want to have a conversation, he hadn't the slightest clue how to make her feel better. Even though he wanted to. He wanted to make *everything* better for her, give back her normal life, and then disappear from it himself. Somehow he felt like he was part of the reason she was so upset.

He should go back outside.

He'd taken a seat at her kitchen table, but now he pushed the chair back and stood. "I should probably..."

"I want to help." Piper turned toward him and spoke, her voice firm and decisive. "I shouldn't have asked to come home tonight. I should have stayed there. I want to help."

"Help...?" Judah thought he understood but didn't want to assume.

"With the case. I want to help you figure out who is after me and why and make sure it goes away as soon as possible so I can get back to my old life."

Not what he'd been expecting to hear, but... "Okay." He nodded. "You can help."

"Why are you standing?" she asked now with a frown. What was he supposed to say to that? Admit that he had no idea how to talk to her? Or should he just leave?

Then again, running away accomplished nothing.

"To be honest, I don't know. But I don't know why I'm in here in the first place."

"Because I asked you to have coffee with me because I can't sleep, and you're a gentleman." Piper poured the coffee into a mug and handed it to him. "You can go back to your car. Or your house. I'm really okay, Judah." She considered him for a minute, almost looked like she was contemplating asking him something. Or saying something.

"What is it?"

She shook her head. "Nothing. Really."

It was the kind of "nothing" that always actually meant "something." Judah waited. Piper sighed.

"Can we be friends?" she asked.

It was the last question he'd have expected her to ask, and somehow for Piper, it made perfect sense.

"Yes." He answered without thinking and then wondered at how quickly the word had come. But why shouldn't they be? Judah didn't want to date anyone, but she wasn't asking that anyway, nor was he full of himself enough to think she might want to. She was asking for friendship and he could give that.

Right?

He had acquaintances. He spoke to his brother, mostly, if he had to talk to anyone about anything.

"Good." She looked relieved. "So if we're friends, can I talk to you about something? Here, sit back down."

He did so and she sat across from him at the table.

"So, someone is after me."

He nodded, recognizing her tendency to process out loud, from the brief time they'd spent together so long ago. They'd met climbing, spent weeks climbing together, getting to know each other, just as friends, eating out, like friends did, and it had been starting to grow into more, the attraction between them mutual, when Judah broke it off.

"How am I supposed to handle this? You're a police officer. You're used to this kind of danger. As a friend, can you tell me how to do this and not panic?"

"I don't know," he started, feeling like that answer was honest all by itself, but wanting to give her more to work with than that. "It's just something that happens in my job and I deal with it when I have to. But, Piper, it isn't your job and, like you were alluding to earlier, it's totally unexpected. Maybe go a little easier on yourself."

She sat up straight, raised her eyebrows. "You're telling *me* to go easy on myself?"

"You heard me."

"You should listen to your own advice, you know."

Judah didn't know what to say to that. Sure he expected a lot from himself, but his job demanded it.

Piper shook her head. "You act half-afraid of me, did you know that?"

He didn't know what to say to that, either.

"Look, should we just get it all out in the open? Yes, we thought about dating ages ago. We hung out. We were friends. We…kissed."

She stopped and he wondered for half a second if she was reliving it the way he accidentally was.

It had been far and away the best kiss of his life.

"But you didn't… We…" She took a breath and he watched her controlled facade fall back into place again. "That wasn't something that continued, so now we are friends, and I'm going to help you figure out who's after me. So can you please just loosen up? I promise I'm not going to kiss you again." A hesitant smile inched across her face, which only made his attention go to her lips. Her soft, full lips that he knew all too well could draw out feelings in him that he'd never experienced before or since.

That promise she'd made, not to kiss him again…

He wished he liked that reassurance.

Judah took a long sip of coffee, burning his tongue in the process, but maybe it was good. It kept him grounded in reality. The middle of the night was a fine time to have a conversation with someone who'd been through trauma and needed an ear. It was a lousy time of day to have a conversation about why you didn't date someone.

Especially since...

Well, it sounded almost like she regretted that nothing more had happened between them. And if he was honest with himself, Judah did, too.

And that was almost scarier than the thought of coming face-to-face with whoever had attacked her. He didn't do vulnerability, didn't put himself into situations that involved risk like the risk you had to take to love someone and let yourself be loved by them.

"I'll loosen up. And you don't have to...promise anything." Judah widened his eyes as soon as the words came out of his mouth. "I mean... I didn't mean you did have to kiss." He trailed off as Piper's laughter erased the awkwardness of what he had said.

"You're fine, Judah. Okay, we're good. I feel better about that."

"Think it's time for you to try to get more rest?" he asked, because he didn't want her to be tired, but also because he felt like he needed to go back to his car. Being around Piper was exhilarating, but it pulled his attention away from where it needed to be, which was on keeping her safe.

"I should try to sleep, yes." She took the empty coffee mug he handed back to her. "Thanks for talking to me. For being here. Thanks for all of it."

He smiled at her, the years falling away. For a second, she was the woman he'd met at an outdoor rock-climbing crag, who had impressed him with her guts and her grace, and he felt almost like he had a second chance.

Surely God knew he didn't intend to date anyone anymore? He'd seen what heartbreak could do to a person, when his brother got divorced. It seemed like Levi's commitment to his job had a lot to do with the demise of his first marriage, and Judah had decided then that if he had to pick, he picked his work.

Now he wondered if that had been a foolish choice.

Levi had fallen in love again and seemed to be living happily ever after. He was still a cop. It was working for him.

But in their line of work there were no do-overs. There was no room for mistakes. And Judah didn't trust himself to do the job well and try to maintain a relationship.

"You're welcome." He smiled sadly, feeling almost like he was saying goodbye all over again as he walked away. "Good night, Piper. Sleep well."

FOUR

Piper had been so sure she wouldn't sleep at all after that awkward, tension-filled conversation with Judah, but she'd gone back to her room, and either the relief of getting her thoughts off her chest, or the knowledge that he was in the driveway, doing his best to keep her safe, had allowed her to relax into some of the best sleep she'd had in a while.

Now it was morning, and she was downstairs, awake enough to think through all they'd talked about, to wonder if she'd imagined the sadness on his face as he walked away. She'd always assumed when he broke things off between them that she had done something wrong, but now she wondered. What *had* happened? Maybe she'd get the chance to ask him, now that they would be working together. Piper thought about it as she brewed coffee, then poured two mugs of it and walked to the front door. Surely Judah would want some after staying awake all night.

But when she walked outside she found that Judah was gone.

So Piper went back in, locking the door firmly behind her because daylight had not chased away her fears. She drank both cups of coffee. There was no reason to be upset, she reminded herself, rolling her eyes at her own disappointment. It was morning now, and she wasn't in an isolated area of the wilderness, so Judah must have decided she was probably safe enough. And she agreed with him.

She wasn't afraid here, not now. At least not *too* afraid, with the door locked. But she did miss him.

Ridiculous.

Also, she wasn't sure how to proceed. They'd discussed last night the possibility of her helping with the case, but Piper was even more aware in the cold light of day of how unqualified she was to assist in any way with real investigative work. But there had to be something. Even if she just went through files and helped organize potential threats...

There had to be something. And Judah had seemed fine with the idea of her helping. So why wasn't he here now? Telling her what their next step was?

Of course he'd have to go home, she told herself as she started up the stairs, making a plan for the day, putting items on her mental to-do list. Coffee, check. Now she'd shower, get dressed and go straight to the police department. She wasn't hungry enough for breakfast and she was eager to get started on doing something to help solve this case. For all she knew, another officer would be the one primarily working her case and she'd seen the last of Judah last night.

That thought made her sadder than it should have. Much as he frustrated her, she...well, she liked him.

Like-liked him, as her friends would have said in middle school.

She'd just reached the top of the stairs when the doorbell rang. Hurrying back down, she blinked when she saw that Judah was the one standing there. She was still formulating an intelligent response when she opened the door and he grinned. All thought ceased in the face of that expression. Judah didn't smile like that often. He usually looked more like he was carrying the weight of the world on his shoulders, jaw tight, a small frown between his eyebrows. So when he smiled, it made an impact. One Piper felt all the way to her toes.

The man had the oddest talent for making her feel like an overwhelmed teenager with a crush. But in a good way.

"Miss me?" Judah said and Piper couldn't help but smile back. Awkward as it had been, it seemed their conversation last night, the way she'd dragged the past kicking and screaming into the open and demanded they both acknowledge it, had helped. He seemed lighter this morning. And she felt less awkward. Piper stepped aside so he could enter the house, and locked the door behind him.

"You know I did." She flirted back, smiling in a way that she hoped implied she was kidding. This was how their relationship had been: easy. Judah had seemed enchanted by her ability to keep things light.

And then he'd ended things before they'd really started.

If she had to guess, he was keeping things this way on purpose. This time, she'd take what was offered, enjoy his friendship and not try to take this any further.

But still, seeing serious Judah Wicks, especially now that she knew him better, lighten up like this? It made her want to spend the rest of her life making him laugh.

And appreciating the stability he could offer her.

She shoved that thought away. Too close to things she made it a policy not to think about. The past was just that. Past. Over.

She was an adult now.

"Seriously." Judah's face shifted to match what he said, and it felt like the sun had gone behind a cloud. "You mentioned last night that you wanted to help. You don't have to, but if you still want, I'm offering to drive you to the police station to talk to me."

"You're working the case?"

He nodded. "Of course I'll check in with my boss, have help from some other officers if necessary, but I'm the one primarily looking into it."

Piper nodded, aware she probably looked ignorant as to how all of this worked, but fought to keep her relief from showing that he would be the one investigating her particular case. For some reason she trusted him more than she did anyone else at the department. Probably that vibe of "you can count on me" that he gave off with every steady breath, with the way he stood there, broad shoulders ready to carry someone else's burdens. *Her* burdens.

"I still want to help." Piper widened her eyes. "I would, no matter who was working it, I mean. But you are. So I am. I mean. I…" She rubbed her forehead, dragged her hand down her cheek and shook her head. "I want to help, yes."

"No coffee yet?" he asked.

"Two mugs, actually." Clearly she wasn't cut out for that much caffeine in that short a time. "Let me run upstairs and get dressed and I can come with you."

Judah nodded and Piper hurried up the stairs. In the daylight, she could almost imagine this was exciting, helping with a case. Nothing seemed as scary right now as it had yesterday, but she knew that the way she'd almost separated herself mentally from the trauma was a coping mechanism, nothing more. Eventually her mind and body would have to deal with that. Nothing ever just disappeared.

She'd learned that the hard way after she'd finally broken up with her ex-boyfriend Drew. But that had been years ago, long before she'd even met Judah. She was better now. Healing. Ready to keep moving forward.

Still, the relationship had lasted almost a year and been incredibly toxic. Those few weeks she'd spent so much time with Judah last year had been the first time she'd let herself think maybe she could have a relationship with a guy and trust him not to be a controlling jerk.

Judah hadn't been controlling, and hadn't been a jerk. He just…hadn't wanted to date her.

There was no crime in that. But it had still hurt.

Piper changed into a fresh pair of dark gray climbing pants and pulled on her favorite top—an old workout T-shirt she'd gotten at a bouldering competition in Anchorage years ago. Then she grabbed a sweatshirt. She'd want it if there was a breeze. Not that they were planning to be outside. But if there was one thing she'd learned over her years living in Alaska, it was that one should always dress for all contingencies. There was nothing worse than the sun coming out, the mountains calling you to come explore, and realizing you had on the wrong shoes and had to go home and change. Piper preferred to always be ready for adventure.

She hurried back down the stairs to Judah, who was waiting in the living room.

"You're ready?" He blinked back his surprise, not covering it very well, and Piper laughed. "What, because I'm a woman I take forever to get ready? You don't know me well enough to assume things like that about me."

She could almost read his mind as she watched him sober quickly. He didn't know her well enough. He could have, but he'd decided not to.

Hadn't wanted to. And there they were, back in the same awkwardness of last night.

She cleared her throat. "Let's head out, then, okay?"

Judah nodded, opened the door for her, and they walked to his car.

Piper took one deep breath, then another, trying to calm her nerves enough that she could get through today. She wasn't asking for a superhuman ability to ignore her doomed attraction to Judah. Just the steadiness to stop making a fool out of herself. Maybe the ability to make absolutely no impression at all, since it was that or a bad one.

They didn't say much on the drive to the station. Judah wasn't a car talker, and Piper didn't seem inclined to speak much this morning, either. He didn't know if

that was normal for her or if she was still bothered by
what had happened yesterday.

Well, of course she would be bothered. Someone
wanted her dead, and that was undeniably bad. But
Judah couldn't tell if her awareness of that was keeping her from carrying on a conversation or if she just
didn't feel like it this morning.

When they pulled into the familiar parking lot—
where, less than twelve hours before, she'd had bullets
flying at her—Judah saw her tense. So, after they were
parked, he came around to her side, opened the door
and then tucked his arm around her while they hurried inside. The way she nestled into him told him she
appreciated it, even if she did jump away from him as
soon as they were inside, as though she'd been burned.

Maybe she had been. Maybe they both had.

They'd walked straight to the conference room of
the police station and then Judah had left to get the
files they needed. When he returned, he stood in the
doorway of the conference room and studied Piper for
a second. Piper sat alone, looking at the blank wall of
the conference room, tapping her fingers on the chair.
Her mouth was set in a firm line, her jaw tense. Her
expression said she would rather be anywhere but here.
But she *was* here. Why? Judah knew Piper was the kind
of woman a man could spend a lifetime trying to figure out. It was part of the reason, too, why he'd been
attracted to her in the first place. She wasn't a stereo-
type, didn't seem quite like the type of person anyone
expected her to be. It made her difficult to get to know.

He'd only left her alone in the room for about five

minutes. He'd had to go up to the front desk and meet Jake Stone, the head of Piper's SAR team, to retrieve the files he'd wanted to take a look at. It seemed Raven Pass SAR was a little behind the times with its records. While they'd started digitizing some things, most of their past case reports were still hard copies.

"I've got the files, Piper," he finally said, softly. She jerked to attention, her petite shoulders straightening.

She nodded. "Good. I'm ready."

Judah needed to make himself stop noticing details about her that weren't pertinent. For example, it was okay to notice that she seemed tense. It wasn't okay to wish he could wrap his arms around her, hug her in hopes that would help her anxiety disappear. He needed to see how she was handling this emotionally, not push her to help at the expense of her mental health, just like he would with any civilian who was helping in this sort of capacity. He did not need to notice the particular blue of her eyes, the way they were warm and drew him in. He did not need to remember what it had felt like to have her eyes focused on him, her laughter, way back when they'd first met by chance climbing—him experienced, her just starting out in the sport.

He needed his focus purely on this case. And as many times as Judah had been accused of over-compartmentalizing in his life, he needed to employ that skill right now. Piper just made it more difficult for him. Her involvement made this case automatically feel personal.

Not so personal that he couldn't work it objectively, though.

"Let's look at what you've been up to the last year or so."

Sure, saying something like that was compartmentalizing at best, didn't at all allude to the fact that they'd lost touch. *Nice, Wicks. Very nice.*

She stood up, motioned toward the box of files he'd carried into the room. "Those are the cases I've worked?"

Judah nodded.

She shook her head. "Why?"

Judah couldn't remember how much detail he'd gone into with Piper the day before, about what he was thinking with this investigation. "I think you keep interrupting someone's plans. I think someone is trying to kill people in ways that look natural, and you are thwarting it when you rescue them. Yesterday seems to have been a trap. There was never a climber in danger. The number that called was a burner phone that one of our officers found in a dumpster in town. The entire scenario was invented to get you in a vulnerable position and kill you."

Piper's face was unreadable. She was silent.

While she was a complicated woman, full of all those layers that intrigued him way more than they should, he'd always thought she wore her heart on her sleeve, her feelings on her face.

Now he wasn't sure.

It added another layer, more mystique, strengthening the attraction.

"It's unnerving to have someone twist it around this way, what I'm doing. And even more so to think that this isn't the first time it's happened."

"I'm not sure if I'm right," Judah reminded her.

"You're good at what you do. If this is the first place your mind goes, I'd say there's a fairly good chance you've got it pegged."

He just looked at her, not sure how to respond. She hadn't seen him at work; their relationship hadn't lasted long enough for that.

A small smile inched across her face. "Judah, you taught me what I know about reading a route on a climb, looking for deviations in the rock that might go unnoticed by some people, subtle angles that will provide friction. If you say you've noticed something here, I'm inclined to believe you."

And now he still didn't know how to respond.

Piper's small smile burst into a full grin, her smile like sunshine to him, just like it always had been. "Just say thank-you and tell me more about my case."

He found himself smiling now, the motion more foreign than it had been once upon a time. "All right. The case." He nodded. "I want to look back at what you've been working on for the past year or so."

"Not more than that?"

He shrugged. "We might not need to go back that far. If we can find a pattern in more recent cases, and nothing suspicious in ones further back, that will help us narrow our search down."

"But what you're thinking is…"

"Like I said, you probably keep interrupting someone's attempted murders. Or…" He hesitated and she caught it.

"What?" she immediately asked, shoulders squared like she was ready to face anything.

"Has there been anyone recently…" He paused again. "Anyone you haven't been able to rescue?"

"You don't have to couch things for me, Judah. I have seen a lot more than you think I have." She looked away.

"I know your job is just as gritty as mine."

She nodded slowly and something flickered in her eyes but disappeared just as quickly, and he didn't know what it was.

She'd been referring to her job when she'd talked about having seen more than he thought, hadn't she? Judah knew next to nothing about her past before she moved to town. He knew her favorite ice-cream flavor, the fact that she secretly loved rainy days and that when she was a kid she'd wanted to be a white water rafter in the Olympics.

But he didn't know about…well, everything else.

"So you really want to know if there's anyone who has died before I could rescue them." She stated it like a fact, but he nodded in case she still needed an answer. "Yes."

Piper blew out a breath. "Yeah, there have been a few. Two or three within the last few months."

"Let's start with those."

Piper moved to the plastic filing container, started flipping through it. "How far back?"

"Just get me the most recent ones."

She pulled out three files. "These are from the last few months." She swallowed hard and sat down in a chair, then lifted up the file on top and held it up for him to see. "Start with the most recent?"

"Yes."

FIVE

The three most recent cases where Piper had lost a victim were all fairly straightforward. Judah didn't think any of them looked like foul play disguised as something accidental.

"You've worked a lot," Judah said to Piper, hoping easy conversation would do something to help the tension he could see building in her shoulders.

"Yep." She answered without looking up from the folders she was paging through. "It's my job."

"People must get themselves into situations they can't handle a lot," he commented.

This time she looked up, her eyes flashing fire. Then she blinked, looked away. "Sometimes it's beyond their control, I'm sure. Not everyone who needs to be rescued is responsible for the trouble they're in. Sometimes people just make a bad choice and it has consequences."

Okay... Judah wasn't sure they were still talking about search and rescue work. If ever there was a comment that deserved a follow-up, that was it, but it wasn't Judah's place to ask and he didn't think Piper was going to volunteer the information. Suddenly, though, he wished they weren't working this case, that it was a rainy afternoon and he could ask her out to coffee and ask that question and others. Why SAR work? Why had she agreed to climb with him immediately when he had met her? What made her trust him?

Just then she shut the file and stood. "I need to go for a walk. Stretch my legs a little."

"Not alone."

She raised an eyebrow, as though slightly amused by how emphatic that response had been. "I had been planning to ask if you thought it was a safe enough idea, but I have a feeling we're going to be sitting here all day. I need a break and some exercise."

He couldn't argue with that. Instead he stood also, motioned for her to precede him out of the room, and locked the door behind them.

They made their way through the police department quickly. Judah wasn't much the type to stop and talk to people when he had something on his mind, but he did give a few smiles and nods in the direction of coworkers who looked up as they walked by. He didn't try to be rude or antisocial or anything like it. He just didn't need to be surrounded by people talking all the time the way his brother seemed to need to.

When they reached the outside, Piper lengthened her stride. It wasn't quite a power walk, no hands pumping up to her face in fists, but it was quick. Judah hurried to catch up, then matched her pace. She said nothing. Neither did he. The summer air was cool on their faces. The sun was shining. It was probably a nice, normal day for a lot of people and it would be so easy to pretend that it was for them, too, to pretend that Piper had just wanted to take a walk with him…

Judah shoved that thought away. *He* had been the one to end whatever was between them. There was no reason to look back and wish he'd made different choices. What was done was done. Now all they could do was move forward. Piper had been right to bring up the past and ask if they could be friends. And that was what Judah needed to focus on: being her friend.

Well, and first and foremost keeping her alive and figuring out who didn't want her to stay that way.

They passed by the library, a coffee shop, some parking lots. She was heading toward the edge of town and he followed her in that direction. She took a trail that led down to the river and Judah glanced down at his fitness tracker. Over two miles so far.

"Are we ever going back to the station or just running away?" he finally asked.

"I just…" She slowed her pace. Shook her head and looked toward him but didn't quite meet his eyes. "I needed to think."

She walked toward the river and sat down on a rock. Judah followed. Fourteen-Mile River rushed by in an angry current. There weren't many things that scared him, but rivers in Alaska were one of them. Unlike some of their Lower 48 counterparts, there was rarely anything lazy or peaceful about the rivers here. They were mostly a glacial, gorgeous blue and filled with heavy silt, moving at a pace that most grown men couldn't stand up against. It wasn't unusual for someone to be lost to Fourteen-Mile River every couple of years. Piper sat fifteen feet or so from its bank, staring at the water.

Could he ask her what was wrong? No, he didn't know her well, but that was the kind of thing people asked generally, right?

"You okay?" he inquired, hoping he kept his voice casual enough that she wouldn't feel he was prying.

"Not really. Looking at those cases is hard, you know? Every single time I go out on a call, I know I could lose someone and let someone down. The cases we are looking at…they were really close. And some of them I failed. I hate to fail. I don't want to be a failure."

Her voice was almost despondent. Judah knew she was good at her job, but no one was perfect, and first responders weren't superhuman. They could only do as much as they could do. He'd lost a fellow officer at the start of his law enforcement career. And he'd seen people die minutes before police were able to arrive at a scene. He knew what it was like to ask "what if," to wonder if there was anything he could have done differently to give another outcome.

He knew what she meant, what she felt.

But what was there to say to that? Judah reached a hand down, almost out of instinct, and patted her shoulder, surprised at how naturally it came to him, to touch her.

Piper didn't jump at his touch, didn't shift away. Instead she looked up and smiled. "Thanks."

He left his hand there a second longer. Nodded and then moved it away. "You're welcome." He waited another second, then spoke. "You know, Piper, in our line of work, I think we need our faith more than ever."

She looked at him. Waiting. He continued.

"We aren't God, Piper. We can't save people, not really. All we can do is be where we are supposed to be, and let God work through us. Our responsibility is to be willing to let Him use us. But He saves them."

She nodded, and they sat in silence for another few minutes. Finally, Piper exhaled, stood. "Thanks, Judah... We should get back, I guess. Go try to figure out which cases have me in danger."

Judah wanted to tell her not to worry about it, that he would do it on his own. She looked emotionally spent. But her perspective was what was going to help them narrow their focus to cases. What had she noticed during certain rescues? What had seemed off? Things like that would find them answers sooner than anything, and for that he needed Piper.

Ideal or not, they were a team for now.

Besides, she had wanted to help and something told him Piper needed to know that she had an active part in this investigation and that she wasn't just a victim. That word and Piper didn't even fit together in his mind.

"Yeah, we should." He let out a breath, trying to remove some of the tightness from his shoulders. He wasn't sure he'd managed to relax them since he'd seen Piper nearly fall off the cliff yesterday.

She offered a small smile and started to walk. "Sorry about the break."

"What about it?" He looked over at her. She wasn't looking at him, but she looked almost embarrassed. Judah didn't know what she could possibly feel bad about. He understood her needing to step back after what they'd been reading about for the last while. Sometimes in the middle of a case he needed to get away for a few minutes, to process.

"Needing it, I mean. I need to toughen up a little more than I thought, I guess."

She didn't sound like herself. There was a hesitancy, a lack of confidence, that wasn't characteristic of her.

"You don't need to apologize for anything. What we're asking…what I'm asking for—help looking for what might have started this—would be hard for anyone."

She started to brush off his words, he could tell, so Judah stopped. Waited until she halted, too, and faced him.

"I'm serious, Piper. Don't apologize."

She studied him for a second, must have decided to believe him. Because she nodded once and kept walking.

And Judah was left wondering what made her feel that way. And made him think there had never been another woman who fascinated him quite like this one did.

They'd been poring over case files for hours, broadening their search from just cases where Piper had lost a victim, to all of the times she had been called out on a rescue over the last year. The walk had revived her some, but it still looked to Judah like Piper was much more tense than normal. She wanted to read through the notes on every rescue in their entirety, in case something jogged her memory, she said, so the process was taking longer. He didn't blame her for wanting to be thorough. At the moment this was the best chance they had at figuring out who was behind the attack on her, and she didn't want to lose this opportunity to find a lead to chase. So Judah had called in a pizza order for lunch and they'd eaten that, then started looking at cases again.

He was starting to wonder if this was like looking for a needle in a haystack. Or something comparably hopeless.

No sooner had the negative thought crossed his mind than Piper spoke. "This one."

Judah leaned toward her, reading what she'd been looking at. The victim had been a thirty-eight-year-old woman named Nichole Richards who had gone missing on a camping trip. Piper and her former teammate Caleb had recovered her body, caught on some branches that overhung the river near the spot where the woman and a friend been camping, according to the report.

"Yeah?" he asked, trying not to put too much pressure on her, but knowing he couldn't keep the hope out of his voice. Especially after hours of nothing.

Piper nodded. "Yes. Her body… I remember her having bruises in several places, including her face, almost like she'd been in a struggle. The ME looked at the body, and while the bruises were premortem, he also thought they were consistent with falling in the river, hitting some rocks." She shook her head. "It just rubbed me wrong. But I thought—" She cut herself off, then started again. "I thought maybe I was reading the situation wrong." The tone of her voice had changed. It was more deliberate. Calm.

Her familiarity with bruises made him uncomfortable, especially when he thought back to last night and the way she'd been quick to apologize, almost berating herself.

Piper was light and fun and carefree.

What had happened to give her another angle to her personality, to make her seem almost afraid of disappointing someone? To make her familiar with bruises that someone would leave on someone else's face?

He couldn't think about that right now, not if he wanted to do a good job on this case. If there was something in her past she wanted him to know about, she would tell him. So he tried not to think about it, and kept his voice steady. "I think you're onto something," Judah said. "May I see the file?"

Piper passed it to him. He read it again, looking for details this time as far as where the body had been recovered, where she'd gone missing from.

"No answers about why she'd left her campsite?"

Piper shook her head. "The friend didn't know where she'd gone. They'd turned in early that night, before ten, and planned to hike the next day."

Judah understood why there hadn't been anything that could be done about it at the time. If the ME said the cause of death was drowning, and there had been no concrete evidence that someone might have assisted that death, there was little evidence anyone could have used to build a case on it. She had no wounds on her neck, so no one had choked her, and besides, Judah knew the ME would have been able to tell if she stopped breathing before or after she went underwater.

But he was confident Piper's instincts were right about this one. Something didn't add up.

"Strange the body was able to be recovered at all," he commented. Fourteen-Mile River emptied just south of Raven Pass into Cook Inlet, a tidal body of water that no doubt hid many bodies and secrets.

"It was amazing. Pure coincidence that her body caught on that tree." Piper shook her head. "The chances weren't good. We just happened to be in the right place at the right time. I like being able to give people closure when I can't save someone."

Or the wrong place at the wrong time for Piper's safety, as the case seemed to be.

"Great, let's set this over here." They'd been through over half of Piper's recent rescue missions. "Need another break?"

"I'm good. You?"

Was she? She'd just reread that entire case file, along with a stack of others, several that he'd seen that had resulted in someone's life being lost. That had to hurt.

Still, Judah wouldn't like it if someone questioned whether or not he could handle something. So he tried to treat her the same way he would like to be treated.

She kept looking through the files, stilled when she looked at one of them.

"That one, too?" Judah asked, moving closer so he could read it.

Piper had cocked her head to the side, considering. "I'm not sure. Maybe? Something about it felt odd."

Judah read the summary. It was a recent rescue. Randy Walcott. Thirty-two-year-old male, canoeing while under the influence, in a lake just north of town. Tragic, but something that happened at least once a summer. Unlike most people, though, this guy hadn't died. The call had come into SAR and Piper had responded immediately, before backup had arrived. It was a violation of protocol, and she'd received a reprimand, but if she'd been any later, the man wouldn't have made it.

She'd risked her job for his life, and it had saved him. And now *her* life might be in danger.

Still, the fact that she'd managed to get there in time was almost uncanny. If someone had fallen into the water, and another person had immediately called 911…

How long would a drunk person have struggled before going under? And how many minutes could he have gone without oxygen?

Even then, the response was too fast.

"Do you think it's weird that you were able to get there and save him?"

"What do you mean?"

Judah stopped. What did he mean? He saw what she did, that something nagged about this case.

"You don't think someone called it in before they'd done it, do you? Maybe just to make sure it looked like an accident?"

Piper frowned. "I don't know. It would explain the fact that he was still alive when I found him."

Judah shut the case file, pushed it toward the other one that had caught Piper's attention, and shook his head. "I don't know… Let's call it a yes for being odd, too."

They kept flipping through. By the time they were done, around four thirty, Piper had found one more that looked suspicious, a rescue of someone who had fallen while hiking and ended up on a narrow ledge. The level of danger and the circumstances felt similar to what had happened the night before. Because of Piper's climbing skills she could rescue the hiker, who hadn't been able to offer a satisfactory answer of how he had fallen. He'd been disoriented, with a concussion, and no foul play had been suspected.

Alone, not too suspicious.

But put together with the other cases that had drawn Piper's attention, and with their newfound curiosity about whether or not someone was after Piper? It was worth looking into.

"Nice job," Judah said. They examined the few remaining files and nothing stood out. They stacked the cases back. That gave him three from this past year to work with, three reasons someone might be after Piper. The more he thought about his theory of why someone might be after her, the more it made sense. But why would someone want to kill multiple people in the town? And in similar ways? A serial killer wouldn't generally focus his attention on anyone but his intended victims. At least, Judah didn't think so. This felt more to him like…well, almost like a hit man, but this was Raven Pass. Was he taking his suspicions too far? He didn't know anymore. He shook his head and went on. "So… next thing I was thinking…"

"Was it that you wanted to take me to dinner and feed me because I've been locked up all day helping you?"

It hadn't been, but her teasing voice, her sparkling eyes caused Judah to almost forget all the reasons that letting himself fall for her would be a terrible idea.

"That's an even better plan." He found himself grinning. When was the last time he'd smiled like that?

"Perfect." She stood up. "I want a steak. Ready?"

He wasn't sure he was, or really could ever be. To take out someone like Piper? Spend time with her outside of the police department and not act on any of the attraction he had to her? Yeah, it sounded like a losing proposition from the get-go.

But time with her was like time outside, refreshing. Unexpected.

Impossible to say no to.

"Steak. I'm ready. Let's go."

SIX

High Tide Steak House was situated near where Fourteen-Mile River emptied into Cook Inlet. It was a restaurant as full of contradictions as Alaska itself, where you could easily find someone in a little black dress on a date, or someone in Carhartt coveralls wanting a good meal after a hard day's work. Looking around, Piper would qualify herself and Judah as somewhere between the two extremes. Not overly dressed up, but not too casual, either. They fit in fine.

Her heart was pounding a little harder than usual in her chest. Had she really asked Judah out? Sure, it was half a joke, and they had been working together all day. This should feel no different than eating pizza together at lunch, right?

It did, though, and she would be fooling herself to try to pretend otherwise.

"I haven't eaten here in forever," she said aloud, suddenly finding herself grasping for some kind of small talk.

"It's good. Great steaks." Another smile from Judah. For a man who seemed to walk around town in a perpetually serious mood, he'd smiled a lot today. Piper didn't remember him being so serious when they'd first met. Actually, he'd been a whole lot less quiet. Less tense.

Piper was suddenly at a loss for words.

The server came, led them to a table by the window. The view was gorgeous but she found herself hesitating when the waitress asked if it was okay. She glanced at Judah.

He nodded. "This is good, thanks."

Piper hadn't been sure. Nothing had happened since she was shot at in front of the police station. But someone had tried to kill her. Twice. A fact that couldn't be avoided no matter how much she might prefer to avoid it.

Still, Judah hadn't been worried about their seat next to the window exposing her to danger, so it would be fine.

Right?

She pulled her chair out, sat down and did her best to ignore the window. Judah sat down also and cleared his throat, then started to talk.

"Listen, Piper."

His voice was low. She could listen to it all day. Piper blinked. Somehow, in the last half hour, the stress of the day had started to overwhelm her. She was tired, and her exhaustion was manifesting itself in a general lack of defenses and no guard up to protect her from her still-present attraction to Judah. He might not have wanted to pursue a relationship when they'd first met a year ago, but Piper had. Truth be told, she'd probably still be interested if he asked.

Wouldn't she?

No, maybe not. Not after the attacks yesterday. She'd known what the police faced. It wasn't that she was somehow unaware of the dangers of that profession. But until she'd had her own life put in danger, not by the wilderness but by people who meant to harm her, she hadn't considered the evil they were up against every day. Loving a cop would mean opening her heart to hurt. And it had had quite enough of that to last a lifetime.

"Piper?" Judah asked. Right. He'd been talking or had been about to say something and the sound of his voice had sent her off into her own world. Pathetic. Maybe adorable, if she wasn't the one being ridiculous.

"I'm sorry, I missed that," she said with a small laugh.

Great, she sounded nervous. Probably looked nervous, too, judging by the amount of tension she could feel in her body.

"I was just saying that we're going to be spending a lot of time together, so I'm glad you suggested dinner."

She blinked, tried to analyze the entire situation. Judah's shoulders were where they belonged and he was leaned slightly back, all of which gave the impression he was not about to jump out of his skin like she currently was.

He couldn't be asking her out. They were already out. And it didn't matter if it was a date or not.

"I wanted to make sure we went ahead and cleared the air between us. I know you sort of did last night, but I just wanted to make sure... No hard feelings?"

No...hard feelings?

The walls went back up, old hurts threatened and

Piper swallowed hard against the familiar questions. Was something wrong with her? Was she doing something wrong? She was twenty-nine. Not old at all, but at an age where she'd always imagined herself in some kind of committed relationship on its way to marriage. Maybe already married, if she were honest.

"Oh, sure," she heard herself say in a tone more casual than she felt. She smiled, knowing it might not have quite reached her eyes, but hoping it was convincing enough. It usually was. No one ever noticed when it covered up how she was really feeling.

He looked relieved.

"So…" She trailed off, struggling for conversational topics. This was painful. Awkwardness made her feel all cringey and all she wanted was to go home, snuggle with her cat, do some yoga and sleep for a long time. The last few days had been too much.

She'd made it through another time that was worse, though, so she could make it through this, too.

Piper took a deep breath and found a conversational topic. "Done any good climbing lately?"

It had been what they'd mostly had in common when they'd met. And it was something that most climbers she knew could talk about for hours with no interruption, unless that interruption was to load up in someone's van and hit the crag right then.

Judah nodded. "Some. I don't have a lot of climbing partners, so I've mostly been going alone."

"Self-belaying?" she asked to confirm.

He laughed that time. "Yes. I don't free solo. Won't ever. It's too dangerous."

Piper agreed with him now. There was a time in her

life when she'd dabbled in climbing without a rope, but that had been years ago. She recognized now that it had been done during a time in her life when she hadn't had enough to live for. She hadn't wanted to die, she knew. She just…hadn't cared enough to care. It had been just after she'd broken up with Drew and she'd felt abandoned by everyone, maybe even by God. It wasn't until later that she realized she'd been the one to walk away from those relationships and had started moving back toward them.

The amount of times God would forgive her and welcome her back never ceased to amaze her.

"Good," she said in response to his answer, not wanting to dwell on that topic. "Any routes I might have overlooked that you want to tell me about?"

Judah started talking about some sport climbing he'd done up north of Anchorage, in the Hatcher Pass area, and Piper listened. As she did, her body started to relax and things felt more normal.

Maybe she could do this after all, keep her feelings under wraps.

Dinner was served and they ate. The food was delicious as always. They were debating dessert when something caught Piper's attention. Movement out the window? Maybe. She looked through the glass but didn't see anything obviously out of place.

A chill ran down Piper's spine. She stared out at the view. The 1964 earthquake had sunk some of the land near here, and it had fallen below the water table. That had killed several trees, and some dead ones were still standing. A memorial of sorts to the devastation that had once overwhelmed this gorgeous place. The mountains in the distance were dark green shadows begging to be climbed, or at least it had always seemed that way to Piper.

This scenery had always comforted her. It had been the solace she'd needed after her last relationship had gone so, so wrong. And it had been a constant in the uncertainty of her childhood. Alaska was a part of her, and she loved it.

But right now, she did not feel peace. Instead she felt…

Almost watched? Like something was out there, somewhere she couldn't see it. Unease crept from her spine to her shoulders.

"What is it?" Judah asked.

Piper shook her head, her eyes not moving from the window, the landscape. "I don't know." She rubbed her arms, shook her head and tore her gaze away to look at Judah. "I think I'm just nervous. Today was tough."

She couldn't tell if Judah was buying her explanation and Piper wasn't convinced she was, either, but she'd had to try to talk herself out of panicking. It wouldn't do her any good.

"Sure?"

She shrugged. "As I can be."

"Let's finish up and get you home."

Piper nodded, disappointed in herself to have ruined what had been a surprisingly nice evening, with her paranoia. But someone was after her. No amount of nice conversations or delicious food could change that.

Judah drove Piper home, hoping the silence was the companionable kind and not the something-was-wrong kind. Levi would know. Judah had spent more time talking today than he had in probably weeks, and he just needed to get home and have some time alone.

Still, dinner with Piper had been…pleasant. Too pleasant, really. It reminded him of all he wanted and couldn't have. If he had another job, if he were better at relationships, maybe. But he'd chosen his career and wasn't changing it now, which meant the decision to avoid romance was already made. But more than anything, he didn't want to hurt anyone else. Especially someone like Piper, who was sweet and beautiful and seemed to already bear invisible scars someone else had inflicted on her.

Judah still wanted to know more about her past. He really wanted to know more about her in general, but how was that fair? He couldn't keep getting closer to her, acting like he wanted a relationship if he didn't.

He *didn't* want one, right?

When they pulled into the driveway and parked, Judah opened his car door and stepped out when Piper did. "I thought I'd check your house for you, if that's okay."

"Please."

Her tone was more emphatic than he'd have expected. Truth be told, he wasn't even sure he'd expected her to agree, much less with any kind of enthusiasm.

"So, Piper, what exactly did you think you saw outside the restaurant?" He hadn't pushed her earlier, but she'd seemed distracted since then, her perfect eyebrows bunched in a slight frown.

"Nothing. I told you that." She looked over at him, then back forward at the road.

"But…" Judah led.

She sighed. "But I felt like I was being watched. I don't know. That's not really something quantifiable, so I hate to say it's true when I really don't know. I just got the odd sensation that someone was observing me."

She appeared to not want him to be concerned, but why? Did she really doubt her gut instincts or was it that she didn't want *him* too concerned?

See, this was his problem. He overthought things too much, analyzed them down to the smallest detail.

"Come with me but stay behind me." Judah told her. 'Cause he sure wasn't leaving her in the car, either.

She did so without complaint and Judah checked the house. It was clear; no one was there but the two of them.

He found that Piper was just behind him.

Judah blinked, the proximity forcing him to admit just how strong his attraction to her was. He almost expected her to notice, too, to give some evidence that she felt it, whatever *it* was between them, though he didn't know why. She didn't even meet his gaze, just looked away from him and backed up.

"I'll…" He cleared his throat, surprised at the way his heart was still pounding. "I'll have someone sit in the driveway tonight to make sure nothing out of the ordinary happens."

"Okay." It felt like they were back to being professionals in similar industries who occasionally worked together. Not how it had felt like earlier, when they had been something more like partners.

"All right. So. Tomorrow we'll touch base? I'd like to talk to you more about the cases you pointed out today and get a better idea for who was affected and see if any of them tie together somehow."

She nodded. "We can do that. I'll call when I wake up?"

Judah agreed. "Sounds good."

She walked him to the door, smiled a sort of sad smile as he wondered what she had to be sad about.

As for him, he had plenty of reasons, he realized as he walked to the car. He'd mess up more than one time, he suspected, in this friendship. Maybe he'd messed up in the first place by backing off and keeping it as a friendship; he didn't know anymore. Law enforcement wasn't just the career he had chosen; it was who he *was*. He couldn't give that up, but neither could he ask a woman to stand beside him through it. He couldn't ask someone to sit by the front window, looking out, wondering if her husband's cruiser would pull into the driveway or if he'd been killed while on duty. He couldn't ask someone to possibly raise children alone.

But maybe even more heartbreaking, he couldn't ask someone to risk their heart when he wasn't sure he could be trusted with it. He would pick his job over love ever time. It had been true until now and he had no reason to believe it wouldn't be in the future.

Judah pulled out his phone and dialed the Raven Pass Police Department. "Hey, this is Officer Judah Wicks. Do we have someone on patrol tonight who could keep an eye on Piper McAdams's house?"

He heard the clicking of keys over the phone, and a rustle of papers as their admin checked. "Officer Holloway is free."

She was a newer officer, but one Judah trusted. He'd

rather stay himself, but...well, for one thing he'd gotten barely any sleep last night and he wasn't foolish enough to think he could keep that up for long.

Also, something told him he needed to keep as much distance between Piper and himself as he could. He was going to be working with her closely on this case. But he didn't need to spend every moment thinking about her, wondering how her night was going, was she safe, did she wish they'd given whatever was between them a chance...

He shoved her out of his mind again.

Tried, anyway.

Judah put the car in Drive and made his way down the quiet streets to his house. The early August night was finally starting to darken. It was always an adjustment to get used to the returning darkness after the month of June, when the sun shone all night long. Even in August it would never be completely dark, but comparatively, it felt like real nighttime.

Of course, that made him more apprehensive for Piper. Obviously, she was in danger at any time of the day as long as someone was after her. But darkness gave criminals better cover, and it gave them places to hide. He didn't want anything to happen to her.

God, help her have a quiet, boring night, please, he prayed, surprised at how deeply he felt it. Had it been a while since he had prayed with so much sincerity? Thinking back on the last few weeks, he thought it might be true. Longer than that, even, really.

His faith had always been important to him, but Judah felt like he was failing in that, too, lately. Always trying but never quite succeeding in having the strong relationship with God he'd had once.

Judah felt trapped in his thoughts all the way home. Besides going over the state of his spiritual life, he was going over the day, too, second-guessing everything like he was sometimes prone to. One of the hazards of being an introvert. He still felt like he'd made some kind of mistake with Piper tonight, but he didn't know what it was. And he was distracted by her to a point where he was starting to question all of the decisions he'd been previously confident of.

Surely that wasn't right? He'd made his choice and needed to stick to it.

It was too late at night for this kind of thinking, especially the mulling-it-over-and-over-in-his-brain kind, but Judah was an introvert. He was used to living inside his head sometimes.

He parked in his own driveway, took a deep breath and went inside. With any luck, he'd sleep well and not think any more about Piper McAdams until morning.

SEVEN

Sleeping was likely a pointless endeavor. At least, that was what Piper had thought after at least half an hour of tossing and turning.

She'd been just about to leave the bed and get herself a snack when she'd nodded off. She must have, because she now woke up suddenly, aware that she'd been sleeping.

Why had she awakened?

Piper blinked against her exhaustion, her eyes dry and tired. She lay there in the darkness, looked at the sky outside the window. It looked like the blackest point of the night, which at this time of year put it near two o'clock in the morning. Not moving, she kept listening.

A door creaked downstairs.

No one should be inside the house but her.

Immediately her heart rate kicked into overdrive and Piper widened her eyes. Sleep was now the furthest thing from her mind. She had a weapon, but she didn't often use it. It was a 10 mm she'd bought to hike with after being warned by one too many well-meaning friends that hiking without some kind of bear protection in Alaska was asking for trouble. She kept it in a case inside her closet. Was it too far away to get to now? Which was better, to lie still and hopefully remain undetected, or to risk getting the gun?

The gun won out. It wasn't as though this was a normal home invasion type of situation; at least, Piper assumed it wasn't. It would be too coincidental. If whoever was in the house was connected to the threat against her, then they were here to harm her. It was somewhere around two in the morning, and her bed was the obvious place she would be.

Piper moved to the closet, clicked the light switch. Nothing happened. The house remained in darkness. Piper shivered. Not only was someone in her house, but had he shut off the power? Blowing out a breath and trying to stay calm, Piper stood on tiptoe to reach the shelf. Her hands were shaking, she noted, but she managed to grab the case and get it down. She pushed a loaded magazine into the weapon, then chambered a round and took a deep breath. Her heart was still racing, but she managed to take a few deep, calming breaths.

Phone. Where was her phone? She needed to call the police.

Or Judah?

The thought crossed her mind, completely unwelcome. Of course 911 made more sense.

But he *was* the police. And he knew her better.

Piper could roll her eyes at her girlish fantasy of having Judah come rescue her. It was ridiculous.

Still, it was his number her fingertips dialed once she got her phone from the bedside table.

"Hello?" His voice held no trace of sleepiness, but

plenty of alarm. And no wonder; there was no safe reason for her to be calling this late.

"Someone is in my house."

"I'm on my way. Stay on the phone."

Piper shook her head. "I'm going to call 911, too."

"Okay. Stay on the line with them, then."

She didn't know what good that would do, except potentially force someone to listen to her being shot, or worse, but she dialed, whispered the same words to them she'd said to Judah with some more details, and then put the phone down beside her.

Now the waiting. Piper hated waiting, hated the way that the darkness felt as if it was pressing in on her chest, like a tangible enemy who wanted to cause her harm.

The dark wasn't against her, she reminded herself. Piper took a deep breath in, like her counselor had told her to once. Years ago, when she'd first learned to be afraid of the blackness. Then another breath out.

She heard a sound from downstairs, a gentle creaking of the floor. The sound sent chills up her spine and she was forced to confront the reality: this was likely calculated, an attempt to cause her harm.

Or worse.

She stepped into the closet, worked her way past her shoes into the back corner, weapon in one hand, phone in the other.

More waiting. More pressing darkness. More breathing. In. Out. Piper squeezed her eyes shut for a second.

God, help me.

A footstep sounded close and then Piper could hear

breathing. A silhouette moved toward her and she leveled the gun, hand trembling.

The pressure on her chest worsened and her vision blurred. Piper blinked as a wave of dizziness threatened her.

No. No. No.

She'd felt this way a few times in the last few years. It was nothing like those first weeks when she was seeing the counselor. Then, she'd battled panic attacks and a level of anxiety that she hadn't known someone could have.

She couldn't feel this way right now.

The hand holding the gun quivered. She let go of the phone and wrapped her other hand around the weapon, too.

The shadow moved. Too fast. She squeezed but her finger never caught on the trigger. Instead the impact of a body coming at her full force knocked her back against the closet wall. She tasted blood and her tongue hurt—she must have bitten down on it. The back of her head throbbed, too, as he did her shoulder, from where she'd hit it.

Her gun. Where was it?

Everything was disjointed. Confusion. Piper didn't know how much was from her panic attack and how much was from the way the attacker moved. The figure didn't move like a person who was angry. Instead, his movements seemed practiced, like those of a person skilled to disable and kill.

She'd only just recovered from the first hit when the second came. This time it was his arm, which wrapped around her in a headlock, choking her.

She'd felt this way before. This was familiar.

Instead of the panic she would have expected, anger flooded her. Piper threw a punch, felt it land somewhere on her attacker's face. Still, he fought her. She punched again, to no effect, then jerked her knee upward, like she'd seen on *Miss Congeniality* once. Her assailant stumbled, just enough for Piper to push herself up. She was out of the closet, but not free yet.

Twisting her body to the left, she fought to get away.

"Police, freeze!" The shout came from downstairs.

Piper found herself suddenly released, and fell down against the floor.

She heard something hit her window and the sound of shattering glass.

Her attacker had escaped.

"Piper!" Judah ran into the room, every argument he'd given himself earlier about needing to distance himself disappearing in the dark room, as he saw her form crumpled on the floor. A weapon was a few feet away from her.

"Is this your gun?" he asked her.

Piper blinked. Nodded. He reached for the gun, unloaded it and set it on her dresser.

She groaned. It sounded like she was in pain, but she was alive, and right now, Judah would take that. As long as there was hope.

People were what was important in life, he knew with startling clarity. How could he pretend he didn't feel the way about Piper that he did?

He looked over at her. There was a red mark on her neck, already darkening with hints of purple, the beginnings of bruise under her eye, and she was rubbing her shoulder.

Someone had hurt her. Had nearly killed her.

"Where is he?" Judah looked around, realizing whoever was responsible had escaped through the now-shattered window.

Judah hoped with everything in him that the other responding officers would catch whomever had done this to Piper. It was probably best that he wasn't outside helping with the on-foot pursuit. He was in no position right now to be the kind of law enforcement officer he wanted to be. Hot rage at Piper's bruises was building inside of him, and Judah knew that for the life of him, he couldn't promise that he would be able to act appropriately.

He knelt beside her. "Are you okay?"

She was breathing, but not responding to him. She was staring into the distance, eyes open.

Judah racked his brain for reasons she could be in this state. There were absolutely no good ones, plenty of bad ones.

As far as he knew, she'd never been the victim of a crime, which was one of the possibilities on his mental list.

"Piper, you've never... I mean, you've never had anything like this happen before, right? Had someone come after you?"

She shook her head.

During his years of police work, the only other time he'd seen someone respond like this to violence was when they'd seen violence before. Several of those women he was thinking of now had been in abusive relationships.

Could that be why Piper was acting like this?

And why she had never seemed quick to commit, either? Why she hid her feelings behind smiles when she thought no one was paying attention?

Judah hoped for her sake that he was wrong. "Piper, I'm going to touch your arm, okay? It's me, Judah, and you're okay." He laid a hand on her upper arm.

She startled. Blinked and sat up. "Judah…" She trailed off. Shook her head. "He got away. I couldn't… I couldn't…" She broke off and started to sob.

"Hey. Hey, it's okay."

Her tears didn't scare Judah, something that surprised him. He hated that she was crying, and sure, he'd make it go away if he could. In fact, he'd fix the whole world if that would make it so she never had a reason to cry again. But right now he wished for her to know that she wasn't alone, that he was here with her, and he wasn't leaving.

Maybe that was what surprised him the most. He didn't *want* to leave, didn't want to give her space or to claim any space for his own.

What he wanted was Piper and him together. Right here, just present in this moment, even if it wasn't a pleasant one.

"You can do this, Piper. Whatever it is, you can do it. You can get through it." He felt the words even more firmly than he said them.

She took a shuddering breath. Then another. And then she met his eyes. "He got away."

"But you're still here. That's what matters most to me."

She blinked, surprise lining every feature of her face. He was surprised at how easily he could read her. It was almost like her perpetual openness, her smile, was a mask of its own that obscured how she really felt. He'd thought she was one of those easy-to-get-to-know people.

Now he was realizing that was a carefully crafted appearance on Piper's part.

What had she been through to make her like this?

Oh, Piper.

"Let's get to the police station, okay? I'll have EMTs meet us there to check you out, just in case. Then I'll take you over to my brother and sister-in-law's house. You don't need to be alone tonight and I can't stay here with you without someone else in the house. I care too much about your reputation for that. Come on, stand up." There was a fine line between pushing someone too far and not pushing enough. Judah felt like Piper needed to keep moving for now. When they were back at Levi and Adriana's house, he'd talk to her about whatever had made her respond like this to tonight's attack.

"Does your gun have a case?" he asked. Piper motioned toward it and Judah put the gun back in it, and then placed it back on the closet shelf where Piper indicated.

She stood and Judah took her hand. She looked at him and frowned.

As they made their way through the darkened house, Judah noticed that the darker the room was, the tighter she gripped his hand. In the hallways, where there were no windows, she practically squeezed the life out of it. She loosened her grip in rooms with windows, where the orange glow from the streetlight could shine through.

God, whatever broke her, I know You can put her back together.

"Wicks." The voice stopped Judah as soon as he and Piper stepped onto the front deck. It was Officer Cook.

"Find anything?" Judah asked and stopped walking. This time it was he who squeezed Piper's hand a little tighter, wanting to communicate that he was still there. Maybe that even though he needed to stop and ask about the case, she was still his number one priority.

"No sign of the suspect once we got into the woods past the house. I was able to follow him pretty closely up until then, but it's someone who either knows the area well or has scoped it out in advance. We're going to canvass the woods again, look for any kind of evidence that we might not have seen when our focus was on apprehending the suspect."

Judah nodded. He wasn't back on duty until morning. Then he might have a choice to make: Stay with Piper, or work? And worse, work meant helping her stay safe, since he would be investigating her case further, hopefully getting closer to discovering who wanted her dead. But leaving her felt wrong, when he considered the fact that he had done so tonight and something had almost happened.

Had happened. Piper was alive and only had minor injuries, nothing Judah even thought needed a doctor— mostly just some bruises on her upper arm and one on her face. But the emotional toll of what had happened clearly went much deeper.

Tonight had been a failure to protect her and Judah didn't want to let that happen again.

"Sounds like a good plan," he said to Officer Cook. "I'm taking Piper down to the station to get a statement. She won't be back here tonight. I've got a place lined up for her to stay."

"Good idea." The officer's face sobered. "Officer Holloway has a nasty head injury. Someone jumped her while she was walking the perimeter. It seemed well planned, she says."

Judah nodded. He'd wondered what had happened to the woman assigned to Piper's house, but finding Piper and seeing if she was okay had been his first priority. "Let me know what you find."

"Will do."

Judah led Piper to his car, opened the door for her, and then hurried to his side. They drove in silence, with Judah glancing over at her now and then to see how she seemed. Her face had settled into an expression that he could only describe as blank. It gave no clues to how she was feeling, unless in fact she was feeling nothing at all.

That didn't seem like a very good sign to Judah.

He parked the car in the parking lot of the police department, then repeated his earlier steps in reverse, hurried around the car to her door, opened it for her and held her hand as she stepped out. "You're okay to do this, right? Just a brief statement, that's all you have to give, and then I can get to you to Levi and Adriana's." His brother had only gotten married three weeks earlier, but given the fact that he and his now-wife weren't unfamiliar with danger and someone being after them, Judah was confident they'd rather Piper stay there than on her own, with the circumstances as they were.

"I can do it." She squared her shoulders and Judah battled between being proud of her and feeling uncomfortable that she seemed to be putting back on whatever self-protective mask he was starting to suspect she usually wore. She'd clearly been through something and tonight was almost like...

He hadn't put his finger on it until now, but it seemed like a form of PTSD.

He was definitely unqualified to be diagnosing her. Immediately upon realizing the possible magnitude of what she might be dealing with, Judah found himself pulling back inside, wondering if he should find someone else for her to talk to.

"Everything okay with you?" Piper turned to him and asked, then glanced down at their hands and back at his eyes.

Her eyes. Her eyes were the clearest pure blue eyes he'd ever seen. And it sounded like some kind of badly written romantic song, but when he looked into them, he saw the entire world differently. It was like he was viewing it through Piper's hopeful gaze, instead of through one that had become somewhat cynical from years of police work and seeing what people at their worst were capable of. How could he reconcile that, the amount of faith Piper seemed to radiate, with how she'd reacted tonight?

"I'll be okay," he told her truthfully, praying that

they could get through the next little while without too much trauma to Piper.

He hoped he was right, that he would be okay. And even more, he hoped the same about her.

EIGHT

Judah hated every minute of their time at the police station. The officers asked Piper perfectly reasonable questions and she answered them well, but with every one, Judah felt like his heart would break.

What had happened to her in the past that made this even harder for her? Judah wanted to know and didn't. He was afraid of what the answers were.

When they were finished asking her questions, he led her back out to the car and drove straight to Levi and Adriana's house.

"Thanks for giving so many details about tonight. You did a good job," Judah said as they pulled into the driveway.

Piper nodded and swallowed hard against her sandpaper-dry throat. If she was going to tell him, it was likely now or never. Even now, as dawn was just beginning to streak across the sky, she was losing her nerve, the daylight taking them out of that time of night where it seemed logical to share secrets, and more into the brightness that demanded they stay hidden.

"About earlier…"

Judah interrupted before she could even really begin. "Let's talk about that inside, okay? I want to know you're safe and preferably curled under a warm blanket with a hot chocolate before we talk about anything heavy or serious."

She should have been insulted, maybe, that it sounded like he wanted to coddle her, but Piper hadn't been treated that way much in her life, and to be completely honest, it sounded nice. Still, something inside told her to keep it lighthearted, so she teased him. "Can you imagine me trying to give my statement at the police station under a blanket and sipping a hot chocolate?" She grinned, the smile feeling watery underneath her frayed nerves. Tonight had been exhausting.

Judah didn't smile.

Piper felt exposed, like he'd seen too much already, and even though there was no way he could know about her past, it seemed like he knew that truly it was no joking matter. None of tonight was. She'd been terrified, almost hurt, thrown deep back into a panic attack the way she hadn't experienced in years.

Why was her first response to joke about it? A residual coping mechanism, she would guess, similar to her too-bright disposition.

She opened the door of the car and walked with Judah to the front door of the house. Adriana opened it.

"Piper, I'm so glad you're here." Levi's wife sounded genuine, her voice full of concern.

"Are you sure I'm not imposing? I mean, you guys got married what, like two days ago?"

Adriana laughed. "For one thing, you know it's been

weeks. You were there at the wedding. For another, that has nothing to do with the fact that you're in danger. What on earth is going on? Come in." She grabbed Piper's hand and pulled her inside. Judah followed.

"Thanks for letting us come over." He nodded at his brother, who had walked into the entryway only moments later. They shut the door and locked it.

"Can I get you something to drink? Hot chocolate, coffee, apple cider? Come in the kitchen—we can all sit down in there."

Piper was too tired to argue, so she followed, but the idea of rehashing what had happened with a group was almost too much. She felt her expression shift and schooled it immediately.

"If you'll just show me where you keep everything, I can make it. I know you guys must be tired, and you don't have to stay awake," Judah said.

She glanced over at him. She knew he hadn't been reading her mind, but he somehow apparently knew she wasn't up for talking.

Adriana glanced from Judah to Piper, and raised her eyebrows slightly. "Right. Yes, we should get back to sleep. If you don't mind, Judah, Levi will show you where we keep the hot chocolate. I think you've been here enough to know how to work the coffee. I'll show Piper where she's going to sleep."

Piper might not know Adriana very well outside of SAR work, but she knew her well enough to recognize the universal girl code for "we need to talk, away from the men." Still, she followed her down the hall to a cozy bedroom.

"What's going on, Piper?"

Piper sighed. "I don't know… Someone is after me, and—"

"That's not what I mean." Adriana cut her off, holding up her hand as though she could stop the answer that hadn't been the one she was looking for. "What is going on between you and my brother-in-law?"

Piper blinked. "Judah?"

"Yes. That's my only brother-in-law, and the only man out there who looks at you like that."

How did he look at her? She wanted to know now, but didn't quite have the energy to ask, and the entire conversation felt too much like it had the potential to take an entirely middle-school-ish turn.

"I don't know," she answered truthfully.

Adriana studied her, like Piper's eyes might hold an answer that Piper didn't know herself.

"He's not a man who treats relationships casually," Adriana said, as though Piper hadn't been able to piece that together from their start-stop-what-was-happening relationship.

"I know."

Adriana nodded. "I've bothered you enough for tonight. I know you're exhausted. You can stay here as long as you need to."

"I appreciate that," Piper said, blinking tears out of her eyes. She didn't even know why she was crying.

"You're going to be okay. I saw the way he looks at you, Piper, and you may not know what is going on, and frankly, he may not, either. But there is no way that Judah is going to let anything happen to you."

It calmed something in Piper's spirit to hear it, even

though she already knew it was true. He cared about her. Too much? Was that why he kept pulling back?

"Everything okay in here?" Judah stuck his head in and the bedroom shrunk inside. The proximity to him was distracting.

"I was just showing Piper the room." Adriana stepped out. "Good night, you two. I hope you sleep some, Piper."

And with that Adriana was gone.

"Hot chocolate is ready," Judah said, his voice lower than usual, probably from exhaustion.

"Thank you," she said, and when he'd stepped out of the room, followed him into the hallway.

Judah had put the hot chocolate on a side table next to a couch in the living room. Piper sat down on one end, expecting him to sit on the other.

Instead he sat beside her. "How are you doing, really?" he asked, as though she could think or remember the answer to anything at all when he was sitting this close, almost touching but not quite, and yes, now that Adriana had mentioned it, he was looking at her like...

She was caught up in his eyes, maybe in the moment, too. That was the only explanation she had for the fact that she leaned into him, breath coming quicker now, heart pounding.

Judah's gaze lowered to her lips, and she stared at him, watched as his long lashes lowered and his eyes closed. Piper's fluttered shut just before Judah finally brushed her lips with his. His kiss was soft, gentle. It gave but didn't take, didn't ask for anything. It felt more like love than anything she'd ever experienced before.

He pulled away and she opened her eyes.

She would not apologize for that kiss. And if he did, she didn't know what she would do. Cry, probably, because she was still so overwhelmed and this had added another depth to her emotions.

But he didn't apologize. Instead he leaned in and kissed her again.

The first had been amazing, but it was barely a whisper compared to the second. The second was deeper, his lips exploring hers. Still gentle, still not demanding, but with more passion than she'd expected Judah would let himself feel.

She lost herself in him. Everything about tonight, her past experiences, faded into the shadow of her memory and all that was left was right now. Judah. This kiss.

Piper never wanted to stop.

She shifted in her seat, moving to face him, her arms wrapping around his neck. He was still kissing her, and Piper felt like everything his embrace was saying was what she'd wanted to hear.

Yes, they could have another chance. Yes, he still had feelings for her. Yes, this might be a man who wouldn't leave her heart in broken pieces.

He broke the kiss and Piper fought to catch her breath, blinking her eyes open slowly.

Judah was breathless, too; she could see it in the way his solid chest moved up and down. His eyes looked dazed, like maybe he hadn't meant for that to happen but he wasn't sorry, either.

Her life was in chaos right now. It wasn't the time to start a new relationship, but maybe this wasn't a new one. Maybe it was the restarting of an old one.

Maybe everything would be okay after all.

* * *

Judah wished he could pull together a semi-coherent thought, but all he could get his mind to land on right now was the fact that he'd kissed Piper. And with a passion that he didn't remember experiencing with any woman. Ever. This had been a soul-deep kind of kiss, and Judah was pretty sure it had made promises to both of them that neither of them could keep.

Because, really, even if he decided he wanted to try relationships, try to be the man that Piper needed, he could offer no guarantees of happily-ever-after. Things happened, people changed, and no matter how much sunny, wedding-day promises were meant to be kept, you couldn't force another person to keep them.

Judah wanted guarantees.

So what did he say now? Piper was looking up at him, eyes wide, and he was calling himself every kind of fool for taking advantage of her vulnerability, but also for waiting so long to kiss her.

"We don't have to talk about it, Judah," she said, her voice soft.

He looked at her, waited for her to continue. Did she mean that they didn't have to talk about the kiss tonight? Or didn't have to talk about earlier, the reason she'd shut down after the attack?

She leaned against him, laid her head down on his shoulder, and he felt himself relax. Her proximity was intoxicating, but Judah didn't want to move away, didn't want to worry right now. For one second he just wanted to be the man who lived in the moment.

"About earlier…" Piper trailed off. "I wanted to tell you about why I acted that way." She lifted her head off his shoulders, looked into his eyes. "If you want to hear it?"

"I do." He'd sit and listen to any story she wanted to tell him, just to listen to her soft voice. But also, he wanted to know her more, to know her better. And he had a feeling this part of her story mattered.

She took a deep breath. "I was seventeen when I met Drew Jefferson. He gave me more attention than I'd ever felt in my life. My parents were good parents. It wasn't their fault, but they were busy and Drew acted like I was his whole world." Her voice lowered. "And maybe I was, for a while? All I know is eventually he wanted to be my whole world. And not in a romantic way. I mean, we were…romantically involved. But he got possessive, and he started telling me not to spend time with my friends anymore, not to wear certain colors if he didn't like them, things like that." She cleared her throat, took a deep breath. Judah wanted to say she didn't have to tell him, or that she could take a break if she needed to, but she seemed determined to get the story out in one breath almost. And he didn't want to stop her if that wasn't what she wanted.

But Judah had heard stories like this one before, and he didn't like where it was going.

Piper shook her head. "I thought… I don't know what I thought, but I didn't recognize it as abuse, not even after he started hitting me. Anyway, tonight reminded me of it. It was that same awful, helpless feeling and I don't ever want to feel that way again, but I did tonight. Panicking like that doesn't happen often. It's been ages." She drew in a deep breath. "I'm sort of embarrassed you saw it, but I wanted you to know."

"I'm glad you told me," he said, and he was. "I wish you hadn't been through that." The things he'd like to do to that man... But it wasn't his job to get revenge.

Piper yawned.

"You ready to try to get some more sleep?" Judah asked.

"I'd like to try, I guess." She shivered. "Unless you think anyone is going to attack us here?"

"I highly doubt it. And if it makes you feel safer, I doubt my brother is going to sleep for the rest of the night."

As if on cue, the floor creaked and Levi stepped from the hallway into the living room.

"Everything okay?" he asked, and Piper wondered if it was her imagination or if he was raising his eyebrows, maybe wondering why the two of them were still awake.

And snuggled together on the couch.

"I was just heading to bed." Piper stood up and glanced back at Judah. His smile was soft, his eyes full of caring, to the degree that she had to look away. Could she let herself be loved without wondering if what had gone wrong last time would happen again?

At the urging of her counselor, she'd finally dated a couple of times since Drew. Not seriously, but enough to remind herself that not all men needed to be looked upon with suspicion. Judah was the first guy she felt like she might be in danger of losing her heart to.

"Sleep well," he said, and she smiled, then walked to her room. She sat down on the bed and took deep breaths to try to calm herself down even more. After a few minutes, though, she decided she needed a glass of water. She eased the door back open and walked into the living area, then the kitchen.

Levi was in the kitchen, eating an apple.

"Sorry, I just needed some water. Where do you keep your glasses?"

He motioned to a cabinet near the sink and Piper filled a glass from the sink, then took a long gulp. For some reason she felt weird with Levi now. He was someone she'd worked with before, but not someone she knew well. And she'd been kissing his brother on his living room couch about ten minutes ago, which didn't do anything positive to lower the anxiety factor when talking to him.

"Thanks." She nodded once in his direction and took a step toward her room.

"Wait."

Piper turned back around.

"Are you and my brother… Are you guys dating?"

She shook her head. "No. We almost did once, but he didn't want to date me. So we aren't. No." It was a much longer explanation than had been necessary, which probably made her words less believable. She wasn't lying. They *weren't* dating. But were they involved emotionally to a degree?

She didn't know, but she'd rather not talk about it.

"Listen, he's a special guy, my brother, and I just don't want to see him get hurt."

Piper frowned. "Why would I hurt him?"

"Obviously you wouldn't on purpose. I like you, Piper. Adriana likes you. It's nothing against you—it's just that Judah doesn't casually date. He's serious, and

I'm afraid if this is just a distraction for you that you're going to end up hurting him."

A distraction?

"I know we don't know each other that well, Levi, but I'll tell you right now you're out of line to say any of that. I have no intention of hurting your brother. But he's an adult and he can date or not date or kiss anyone he wants to."

Levi's eyebrows rose. Yeah, she shouldn't have mentioned kissing. But it was late, really early in the morning, actually, and her filter didn't always work that well when she was exhausted.

"I'm glad you care about him, but he needs to make his own life decisions. Thanks again for the water and for letting me stay. Good night." She hurried back to her room before he could say anything else. They'd have to talk again. The police department and search and rescue cooperated too often for her to be on awkward terms with anyone, but Piper just couldn't take any more now.

She'd been so blissfully tired, ready to get some sleep even after all that had happened, but now she lay in the bed, covers pulled up to her chin. Her shoulders were tense and her body was exhausted, but her mind wouldn't stop working.

Was Judah too serious for her? Was she being inconsiderate to him somehow, to…to think of falling in love with him?

Piper knew Levi's concern was brotherly and that he just didn't want to see Judah get hurt. But Piper didn't, either.

Did life offer those kinds of guarantees, though? Wouldn't it be worse for her to worry so much about getting hurt or hurting him that she refused to see where this could go? Piper thought so. That was how she tried to live life now, making sure she didn't have regrets.

Maybe Judah disagreed.

Maybe they should have talked about that kiss after all.

Her thoughts in a storm of uncertainty, Piper closed her eyes and finally fell asleep.

NINE

Judah was back at his brother's house within hours. He'd tried to sleep at his home but had lain awake for the remaining few hours of the night, formulating a plan instead.

The feelings growing in his heart toward Piper told him to keep her away from the case entirely, but logic reminded him that wasn't necessarily the way to keep her safest. Instead, what he'd come up with would put her right in the thick of the investigation. If he was right, then letting Piper get involved was the right thing to do, and maybe the best way to keep her safe.

"You're here early," Levi commented when he eased the door open for him.

"You're awake already? I was going to just let myself in with my key."

Levi laughed. "Seriously?" His face turned serious. "Judah, about this thing…"

"What thing?" Judah stepped inside the house.

"Piper."

"She's not a thing. She's a person."

"I mean the thing you have going with her."

"There's no *thing*, Levi. Say what you mean. Do you have any coffee ready?" Judah felt his shoulders tense. He and Levi had just started getting along better, after years of his brother feeling like he somehow didn't measure up. Levi had never said that to him, but Judah had finally pieced it together from the way Levi had always acted—like he had something to prove. He didn't do that now, since he had met Adriana.

"Coffee's in the pot," Levi said. Judah walked in that direction, found himself a mug and started pouring, not sure he wanted Levi to continue but pretty sure his brother was going to. Levi wasn't one to hold back, and he was a bit of a talker.

"I'm worried about you. You never fall for women the way it looks like you're falling for her."

"And that's a bad thing?"

Levi paused, looked like he was thinking. "Not unless she hurts you."

Judah laughed, but it didn't feel like the kind of laughter that came when Piper said something funny. He'd laughed more yesterday than he had in years, and she didn't even try.

He'd spent time thinking about that last night, too. At first he'd assumed her sunny disposition was who she was. Then he'd thought it was a mask to cover the hurts she'd endured. Now he realized it was all just Piper, a woman who had come through some darkness and still had light and hope left in her.

She was special. And he didn't like how it felt to stand here talking to Levi about her. Had he discouraged *Levi's* relationship with Adriana?

Oh. Well. Maybe he had. But he'd just been concerned about his brother.

Which was probably why Levi was being nosy now.

"Listen, I'm glad you…you know…worry about me or whatever." Judah cleared his throat. It still felt weird to have these kinds of talks with Levi instead of just barking at him. But he was trying. "But I'm fine."

Levi nodded. "Okay."

A door creaked and Judah stepped out into the hallway, where Piper was coming toward him.

"Morning." Judah smiled in her direction.

She looked surprised, either at seeing him or his smile, Judah didn't know, but she grinned back. "Good morning. You're here early."

Judah shrugged, and unless he was imagining things, Piper's cheeks blushed a little. Part of him was amazed that even this morning, in the light of day, he still didn't want to apologize for that kiss last night. He'd worried that when he was fully awake he'd regret it, that all of his conviction about staying out of a relationship and staying unmarried would come rushing back.

Now? All Judah knew was that Piper was the strongest, most interesting, most beautiful woman he had ever met. And if God had placed her back in his path like this, Judah wanted to pay attention, make sure that all his determination not to date hadn't just been him being afraid or taking on responsibilities that weren't his. It was an honorable thing to not want someone to get hurt. But he couldn't give guarantees. It was never supposed to be his job to do so.

Maybe that was part of what relationships were about. Taking the risk to love someone.

He swallowed hard at the *L*-word's appearance in his mind, focused back on today and the plan.

"I have a favor to ask," he said to Piper, wondering how anyone could be so beautiful and distracting in a pair of skinny jeans and a hoodie. She was on her way to the kitchen, so Judah followed her in there. Levi had disappeared, for which Judah made a mental note to thank him later.

Piper started pouring her coffee.

"I could use your help today."

Piper took a sip. Then another. "I let the SAR team know that I needed some time off. I figured you wouldn't want me going out to do rescues."

"I appreciate that." It had crossed his mind, but he hadn't wanted to push. Part of what he liked about Piper was her independence and he hadn't wanted to step on that in any way. But the idea of her continuing to go out and perform rescues, especially when it seemed like someone was targeting her because of those, didn't sit well with him. He'd wrestled with himself about that in the car on the way over today, and he was thankful she'd reached that conclusion without his input.

"I did tell them to call me if it was absolutely necessary and I'd come in." Judah did his best to keep his expression level, since it almost looked like she was trying to decide how he felt about that.

"I don't love it." He shook his head. "But I understand it."

Relief flooded her features and she took another sip of coffee.

"I need you to take me to the sites of the rescues we thought were suspicious."

"What?" Piper blinked, like that was the last thing she'd been expecting. "I think I have you figured out and then you surprise me. Especially after... I mean..." She blushed again. Had he ever noticed how easily she did that? Judah liked it. Frankly, it made him want to kiss her again, but there was a difference between a spur-of-the-moment kiss and familiar kisses in a kitchen.

She wasn't really his to kiss that way.

Judah blew out a breath. "I get what you mean. Yeah, I'd rather lock you up somewhere and keep you safe, so you've got me figured out there."

She laughed a little.

"But honestly I don't know how long this case will drag out and I'd like to keep this investigation as short as possible. To my way of thinking, the fact that some-one is after you is what's most important. Since we have no other ideas as to why you'd be a target, we're working with my theory that maybe you've interrupted some murders by rescuing people."

"Why would someone go to all that trouble to kill people, though? I mean, murder doesn't make sense to me anyway. But if they want someone dead, why not just shoot them?"

"If someone had shot the people we put on that list of suspicious rescues yesterday, how much investiga-tion would have happened?"

"A lot," Piper answered immediately. "Ohhhh."

Judah nodded. "And because it was assumed that these were normal backcountry rescues, they weren't investigated at all."

"That's really...wow, that's more involved than I

would have thought. So, definitely premeditated murders, if we are right."

"I agree. And possibly murders someone has been hired to commit."

"What?"

Judah shrugged. "Just another hunch. It's a very clean way to murder people. Multiple people have died or almost died, even if we are still looking into how... It's an option I'm considering. It could also be a serial killer."

"I still don't know how you do this." Piper shook her head.

"You'll be okay helping out for a short time, right? I know it's not what you prefer to do with your time."

Piper was nodding before he was even done talking. "I don't like it, Judah, but that doesn't mean I'm the type to stick my head in the sand. As long as me helping you with the investigation is making it go faster and getting me out of danger, I'm willing to help how I can. You want to go to the sites of the rescues, and that's exactly what we'll do." She glanced down at her bare feet. "I'll put some shoes on."

"You can eat breakfast."

Piper waved him off. "I'd rather hurry up and get started. I'll be right back."

Judah was left alone in the kitchen. She'd reacted fairly well to the plan, he thought. But he was still concerned about her, and the toll an investigation like this would take.

He'd asked her if she would help and she'd said yes. He needed to respect the fact that she was making her own decisions. If she said she would do this, she meant it.

It didn't stop the feelings of foreboding from pressing down on his chest or the panic that so easily rose in his throat. She was in danger, could be in more because of him.

But they needed whoever was after her stopped. Which meant figuring out who it could be. And why.

Piper's thighs burned from their hike. They'd decided to start with the last case she had found that looked suspicious, the one where the hiker had ended up on a narrow ledge and needed to be rescued. The spot wasn't too far from where she'd been attacked the other night, but it was a different cliff, different victim. To get to the ledge, they'd hiked to the top of Riverview Point, then rappelled down to the ledge. There was some climbing on that wall, but it would take more time than they had. Judah had broached the idea of climbing, but that was something she had good memories of doing with Judah. She didn't really want to mix business, investigating this case, with pleasure.

Of course, she reminded herself around deep breaths, wasn't that exactly what they were doing? She'd managed to push thoughts of herself and Judah to the back of her mind for most of the morning, but now, on the quiet hike, with nothing but the sound of the leaves in the trees and the occasional call of a bird to distract her, Piper found he was on her mind again.

What had made him decide to try again? Or were they even doing that? Maybe he still wanted to be friends at the most and the kiss had been an anomaly?

If that was true, though, it was a heck of an anomaly. Piper could still feel tingles on her lips. It felt pretty likely she'd remember that kiss forever.

Almost to the top, she told herself in an attempt to stay focused on what they were doing and not let herself be distracted by thoughts of Judah. It would be easy to do, and it was critical that she keep her focus out here, for her safety.

Judah was keeping close to her, in case the threat resurfaced. Much as Piper might want to protest because she did like being independent, she knew she needed him. Last night had been too close a call. She had bruises on her as a reminder, and it wasn't like she needed reminding. That had been too close. Piper hated feeling like a victim or like she was in danger.

They made it to the top and geared up, pulling on their harnesses and tying off to the rope. Judah took care of the anchors and got them all set up.

"Ready?" he asked her.

"Ready."

Piper belayed down to the ledge first and Judah followed.

"He was right about here." Piper could remember the scene. The man had been heading toward hypothermia, having been out on the ledge all night. In Alaska, it wasn't far-fetched to assume that before long he may have died from exposure. Or starvation, if he stayed on the ledge long enough. The rock below it was climbable, but not easily, especially without a rope. An inexperienced climber would fall almost immediately.

"What do we know about the guy?" Judah asked.

Piper pulled out her phone. She'd snapped a picture of each of the files that had caught their attention yesterday. "Jay Jones, thirty-one-year-old male. According to the call, someone saw him and it was assumed that he fell while hiking on the trail above the cliffside." Piper frowned as she reviewed the notes. She'd read this yesterday but it hit her even harder today.

"It says the hiker didn't remember falling."

Judah frowned, too. "That is odd." He looked up at the expanse of cliff above them. "Isn't it? You probably know more about the medical side of things than I do, with your rescue work."

It warmed her to see how capable he thought she was. One of the things she'd learned from the whole situation with Drew was that not every man liked that in a woman. She would never again take for granted someone appreciating her for who she was.

"It's possible, especially if they sustained a head injury."

"Do you know if he did?"

Piper shook her head. "Our files are pretty limited. There's not a lot of follow-through. We find people, then we pass them on to the hospital if necessary."

"But we could talk to him."

"We could."

Judah looked at her for a minute longer.

"Let's look at the other locations first."

Piper nodded. "You're the boss."

Judah smiled. "Hardly. You're just helping me out. Which I appreciate."

"I appreciate you being willing to do all this."

"It's my job."

"Oh. I mean, I know." She smiled at him, did her best to keep it light. "But…"

FREE BOOKS GIVEAWAY

2 FREE ROMANCE BOOKS!

2 FREE SUSPENSE BOOKS!

GET UP TO FOUR FREE BOOKS & TWO FREE GIFTS WORTH OVER $20!

We pay for everything!

YOU pick your books –
WE pay for everything.
You get up to FOUR New Books and
TWO Mystery Gifts...absolutely FREE

Dear Reader,

I am writing to announce the launch of a huge **FREE BOOKS GIVEAWAY**... and to let you know that YOU are entitled to choose up to FOUR fantastic books that WE pay for.

Try **Love Inspired® Romance Larger-Print** books and fall in love with inspirational romances that take you on an uplifting journey of faith, forgiveness and hope.

Try **Love Inspired® Suspense Larger-Print** books where courage and optimism unite in stories of faith and love in the face of danger.

Or TRY BOTH!

In return, we ask just one favor: Would you please participate in our brief Reader Survey? We'd love to hear from you.

This FREE BOOKS GIVEAWAY means that we pay for *everything!* We'll even cover the shipping, and no purchase is necessary, now or later. So please return your survey today. You'll get **Two Free Books** and **Two Mystery Gifts** from each series to try, altogether worth over **$20!**

Sincerely

Pam Powers

Pam Powers
For Harlequin Reader Service

Complete the survey below and return it today to receive up to 4 FREE BOOKS and FREE GIFTS guaranteed!

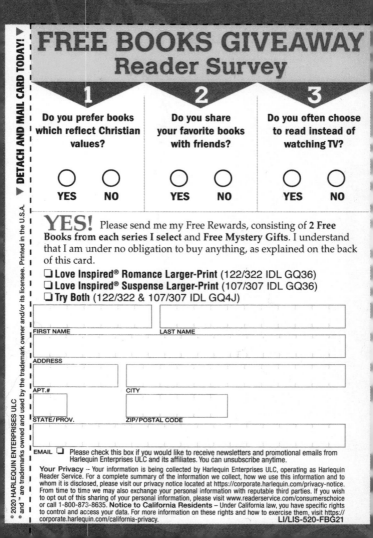

FREE BOOKS GIVEAWAY
Reader Survey

1
Do you prefer books which reflect Christian values?

◯ YES ◯ NO

2
Do you share your favorite books with friends?

◯ YES ◯ NO

3
Do you often choose to read instead of watching TV?

◯ YES ◯ NO

YES! Please send me my Free Rewards, consisting of **2 Free Books from each series I select** and **Free Mystery Gifts**. I understand that I am under no obligation to buy anything, as explained on the back of this card.

❏ **Love Inspired® Romance Larger-Print** (122/322 IDL GQ36)
❏ **Love Inspired® Suspense Larger-Print** (107/307 IDL GQ36)
❏ **Try Both** (122/322 & 107/307 IDL GQ4J)

FIRST NAME   LAST NAME

ADDRESS

APT.#   CITY

STATE/PROV.   ZIP/POSTAL CODE

EMAIL ❏ Please check this box if you would like to receive newsletters and promotional emails from Harlequin Enterprises ULC and its affiliates. You can unsubscribe anytime.

Your Privacy – Your information is being collected by Harlequin Enterprises ULC, operating as Harlequin Reader Service. For a complete summary of the information we collect, how we use this information and to whom it is disclosed, please visit our privacy notice located at https://corporate.harlequin.com/privacy-notice. From time to time we may also exchange your personal information with reputable third parties. If you wish to opt out of this sharing of your personal information, please visit www.readerservice.com/consumerschoice or call 1-800-873-8635. **Notice to California Residents** – Under California law, you have specific rights to control and access your data. For more information on these rights and how to exercise them, visit https://corporate.harlequin.com/california-privacy.

LI/LIS-520-FBG21

▼ DETACH AND MAIL CARD TODAY! ▼

Printed in the U.S.A.

® and ™ are trademarks owned and used by the trademark owner and/or its licensee.

© 2020 HARLEQUIN ENTERPRISES ULC

⬦HARLEQUIN® Reader Service —Here's how it works:

"It is more than that. This time." He stepped toward her, admitting out loud what Piper had already suspected.

Again, she felt the energy between them, something that went so much deeper than just the word *chemistry* could convey. It was more than physical attraction, although Piper felt plenty of that. This felt scary, like it had the potential to change her entire life.

What would it be like to love Judah Wicks without holding herself back?

Piper stepped forward, too, lifted her face almost without thinking.

Judah brushed the slowest, softest, most perfect kiss across her lips, then just stood there. His hands had come around her waist and she hadn't noticed till now as he stared into her eyes.

He was the kind of man she never would have imagined she'd fall in love with. After the abuse she'd suffered at Drew's hands, she had always expected that she'd have one of two problems with romance. Either she'd only be attracted to men with no leadership qualities, that she could walk all over, because that was safe. Or that against her will she would keep falling for men who were abusers, because it was an easy cycle to fall into and a difficult one to get out of.

Instead she'd done neither. She was falling for a man who was a leader, but who cared about her. A man who was probably stronger than any man she'd ever been interested in, but who treated her with the care of someone wanting to keep her safe above all else.

She liked it. She felt…cherished.

But oh-so vulnerable.

Piper cleared her throat. "We should go to the next site." Her voice was soft and low.

Judah nodded without breaking eye contact. "We should."

And somehow Piper knew if she stepped forward again they wouldn't leave, at least not yet. They could stay right here, just spend the day kissing and talking and forget about the case. Piper ached for it, for a day that was normal, without the constant anxiety hanging over her. But wishing for it wouldn't make it any more real, and it certainly wouldn't help her face what her actual reality was.

The only way through a crisis like this was through it. Piper didn't want the kind of easy-come-easy-go relationship that only distracted her from reality. She wanted the kind of love that would walk through the hard times and help her through it, not pretend they weren't there.

"We need to." Piper looked away from him, double-checked her harness and knots. "Ready to head back up?"

He checked his harness, too, and they went back up the wall. When they reached the top Piper was breathless from exertion, but she still wasn't sure if her elevated heart rate was entirely due to that or if it had something to do with Judah. Probably both.

To keep herself focused, she talked about the case on their hike down. "There are two more sites. There is the lake where a man was canoeing and had an accident because he was under the influence, but that lake is really close enough to the road that we could drive right past it."

"Did they test his blood alcohol, do you know?"

Piper shook her head. "I don't know details like that, but I will tell you he seemed drunk. It wasn't difficult to believe he'd gotten himself into the mess he was in."

"You don't always think that, though, do you?"

"What do you mean?"

"Only that I've mentioned that before, the idea that sometimes people get themselves into trouble and then you guys are expected to rescue them, and you seemed pretty strongly like you didn't agree."

Piper couldn't believe how observant he was. Was it a police officer's intuition, the kind of thing that would make him really good at his job, or was it that he paid extra attention to her, to her feelings and reactions?

"I think…" she started, wondering if she was really going to go into this with him. But she could trust Judah. He wouldn't use information to hurt her or hold against her. Judah didn't use closeness as a weapon. He wasn't the kind of man who ever would. "I think that it's because of my own past. I'm sure there are some people who would say I got myself into the mess I was in by choosing to date Drew." She took another deep breath. "When really the reality is that sometimes people make choices and don't realize they are bad ones until much later. It's that connection that makes me have more compassion with people who end up a little deeper than they meant to be or in a bad situation when they were so sure they had planned for all contingencies."

Judah nodded slowly and his expression said he was thinking over her words. "I can see why that makes sense," he finally said. "Thank you for telling me. You're an amazing woman, Piper."

She felt her cheeks heat. Amazing. Judah thought she was amazing.

Forcing her attention back to the case, Piper reminded herself that while whatever was developing between them was exciting, she still had to make sure she didn't entirely lose her focus. Because right now someone would like to ensure that they didn't have a future together.

Because someone still wanted to make sure that Piper had no future at all.

TEN

After that conversation, they'd turned to other topics, like the case. Judah decided that they would just drive by the lake, but also that they would look into all three instances at the police department, in case there were further records they could follow up on.

"I also want to go talk to the survivors, and maybe the family of the woman who didn't make it, if we can." Piper admired the way he worked a case, the way he seemed just attentive enough to it without being stressed. It seemed to come naturally to him, trying to save the world, and Piper loved him for it.

Or could. Maybe. One day.

It was too soon to consider that word, really. Wasn't it?

"We can do that." She agreed with him, trying to keep her mind on a businesslike track.

Whatever. She was trying to stop remembering how it felt to kiss Judah Wicks; that was the honest truth.

They hiked back down to Judah's car fairly quickly.

"So...the police department and interviews, or the last scene?" Piper asked as they climbed in.

"Honest, I'd like to see where you recovered the

woman's body." Judah looked at her like he was gauging her reaction. "Is that okay? If it's too much for you, I can see if someone else will take me there."

Piper shook her head. "Not a lot of people are going to be comfortable navigating a boat on that stretch of Fourteen-Mile River. That was part of why I was involved in that rescue."

"Are you up for it today? I know we've already done a lot."

He didn't mean it as a challenge, but Piper raised an eyebrow anyway. "I think I can keep up with you pretty well, Judah."

"You definitely can." He grinned.

Maybe that was what appealed to her most about him. He didn't seem like he needed to outdo her. Back when they had been climbing partners briefly, it had never seemed like he was trying to push her too far, or to show off in front of her. He'd encouraged her to do her best and he'd done his and they'd just...matched.

Piper couldn't remember the last time she was so thankful to be wrong. Or the last time she had been so thankful for second chances.

"If we're going to go to the recovery site of the woman who drowned, we're going to need to go to SAR headquarters and get an airboat."

"Is it okay for you to do that?"

Piper nodded. "It shouldn't be a problem. I'll call Jake just to be sure." Jake Stone, the head of Raven Pass Search and Rescue, tended to be understanding about things like this. As long as it wasn't currently needed and she was prepared to take the boat back in the event that it was needed for a rescue, she was fairly certain he would say it was fine.

A quick phone call confirmed that.

"We're all set. The boat is in town at headquarters and we can trailer it to the river and I'll show you."

When they arrived at the building that housed their search and rescue equipment and a small office, Piper got everything set up. Judah helped wherever he could, but this was a dance she'd done many times. So mostly he stayed back and let her do what she needed to do, asking occasionally what help she needed.

It was nice, feeling that they worked well as a team.

When they were loaded, they hitched the trailer to Judah's car. At the river, they put on life jackets and then Piper maneuvered the boat into the water without too much trouble.

Navigating up the river was a different story. The current fought hard, like it always did, and although it was something Piper was fairly used to, she would never say that she was comfortable on rivers like this one. It wasn't just the rapids that made this river a challenge. It was the tide, as well, the extremes with which it came in and went out, the dangerous rocks, and the thick glacial silt that made the water heavier and thicker than a normal river. That was part of what made Fourteen-Mile River so dangerous; someone couldn't fall in and easily swim out. If someone fell in and SAR was called to the scene, it was usually going to be for a recovery, even with a life jacket. The glacial silt pulled people under and ran too fast for someone to have much of a chance of survival. True river rescues were rare here in this corner of Alaska.

"I'm going to run us upriver as far as her campsite," Piper said, loudly enough to be heard over the roar of the fan. "I want you to see where she was staying so you can get a sense of the entire scene."

"Sounds good," Judah shouted back.

They continued up the river, Piper struck as she always was by the bright blue of the water. The river narrowed as they continued. She squinted at the shore to try to remember the exact spot. *There.*

"They were camping right here." She motioned to the side.

"Can we beach it?"

"We can. It'll take some maneuvering because the current is so strong, but…" Piper worked the rudders and within a few minutes had beached them.

Judah climbed out of the boat first, and Piper followed. The wet gravel sank underneath her hiking boots and crunched as they walked up the shore toward the dirt. "The tent was set up right here." Piper pointed. The now-bare grassy spot sat beside a firepit ringed with rocks. It was an ideal place to camp, provided people stayed away from the river, lest they fall in unexpectedly.

It was probably a peaceful place, to anyone who didn't know its history. To Piper, even the soft wind in the trees, rustling the leaves, sounded like a sad song. This place represented failure, to her. There had been nothing she could have done differently to save the woman who had died not far from here, she knew that. But it didn't ease the sting at all. Piper wanted to save them all, and in search and rescue work, it just wasn't possible.

"There was no reason at the time to suspect foul play. The victim—Nichole Richards—seemed to have just gone on a walk and fallen in. It was August, so it was late enough in the summer that it was starting to be dark late at night. It was a story that made sense. The victim had no in-state family, and out-of-state family believed the 'fell in the river' story also. There was an autopsy done, I think I mentioned to you, but it seemed to confirm the assumptions."

"Do you think the ME who did the autopsy refused to see something on purpose or was part of a cover-up?"

Piper was already shaking her head. "You can check out that angle if you think you need to, but no, I don't. There was nothing glaring. It was just with my own experiences… Well, honestly I thought I was letting my own past play too much into my interpretations. At the time someone leaving bruises was almost more plausible to me than rocks leaving them."

"I hate that you went through that."

His voice was low, somewhere between sympathetic and indignant. Piper was almost glad for Drew's sake that he'd moved out of state long ago. Judah, she was fairly certain, would like to put a fist in his face.

"I'm okay now. Don't forget that." She fully believed it to be true. Her past was just that. And yes, there'd been a lot of work and healing that had to take place, but now it was nothing but a bad memory. It didn't affect her life anymore at all. Well, sometimes she still wrestled with the idea that she should have reported him to the police—she hadn't at the time. But besides that, he didn't affect her anymore.

Right? Piper hoped he didn't. But she also knew she

might be fooling herself. Someone didn't walk away from a relationship like that completely unscathed.

"I'll try."

Judah kept walking around. He was taking it all in, Piper guessed. Obviously too much time had passed for there to be much evidence, but he checked anyway.

"Pretty sure in the year since it happened any footprints or anything will be gone," she joked.

"Clothing fibers might not be, though."

He was serious and Piper smiled. The man was intense when he was doing his job. "I hadn't thought about that," she admitted.

He continued searching, walking deeper into the woods.

"I'll just come with you," she muttered as the followed. The last thing she wanted was to be left alone when she didn't have a weapon or any kind of protection with her.

"Where are you going?" Piper finally asked.

Judah turned and looked back at her. "I'm not sure, to be honest. I just noticed this trail and wanted to check it out. It's possible the killer used it to access the camping site."

Not just possible, but likely. The woods near the river weren't so thick that they couldn't be hiked through, but people tended to take the path of least resistance. He was right to look around back here, Piper knew, but she was tired of being here.

Tired of this whole thing, actually.

They walked back to the tent site. Judah was still in investigating mode. Piper looked out across the river, mostly to take her mind off what he was doing. It was getting overwhelming, all of this. Once again, she was reminded that there was a reason she hadn't chosen any kind of investigative career. This was wearing on her, heart and soul. Piper was ready for it to be over.

Judah continued searching the area, making mental notes about how close the river was from the spot Piper thought they had camped, and decided that he wanted to read this report when he got back to the police department.

He glanced over at Piper and found her staring out at the river. He walked in that direction.

"You okay?"

She jumped.

"Whoa." Judah rested his hand on her arm. She looked over at him. Her eyes seemed darker than usual. Like she'd been crying and the color had gotten more vivid.

"Hey, what's wrong?"

At first she didn't answer, just looked up at him, blinking. He felt bad for thinking she was beautiful at a time like this, when she probably would rather have sympathy than admiration, but he couldn't help but notice. It wasn't just her physical appearance. He'd heard that some people's internal attributes made them even more attractive, but he'd never seen how true it could be until Piper.

"This is just more than I'm used to doing. It's a lot." She sighed, frustration evident in the way she scrunched her entire face into a frown. "I hate knowing someone wants to kill me. I hate knowing someone might have murdered a woman here…"

And that she couldn't save her, Judah would guess, was also part of it. But yes, he knew what she meant. This place felt off somehow. Like the landscape itself was sad about what had happened here.

"I've got all I need. We can go if you're ready."

"Yeah, I've got no reason to stay." Piper was back to the boat almost before Judah could follow her there.

She started it up with the same professionalism she had shown earlier. It was still fun to watch her do something she was so good at, though.

He wanted to talk to her about that, about so many other things, but he knew he should stay focused on the case.

"And then where was her body recovered?" he asked Piper.

"Right up here." The boat continued forward. "Right at this point."

Judah nodded. "Okay, I can see where it would have…caught." A branch overhung the river and created a tangle of weeds at the edge.

"Yeah, and…"

Judah heard something snap. Something metal.

His gaze immediately went to Piper.

Her jaw tightened. "This is bad."

"What's bad?"

She was shaking her head, messing with the mechanics of the boat. The fan was still spinning in the back, but their course seemed more erratic than before.

"I can't…"

Piper looked up at him, terror written on her face. "Something's wrong. I can't steer."

The craft was still powering forward, but when she

moved the steering mechanism, the fan didn't respond. The boat dipped down, tossed around in the rapids. Whereas before it had felt like the craft was skimming the top of the water, strong enough to overcome some of the turbulence, now it felt like they were at the river's mercy.

God, what do we do now? Judah half wondered, half prayed. Wholeheartedly hoped for an answer.

They were both wearing life jackets, so that was good. He was trying to focus on the positives, but hurtling down the river toward the inlet without any way to steer didn't exactly lend itself to that.

"This is bad. It's really bad." Piper's usually positive face was stricken, her eyes wide.

"What can I do to help?" he asked, in case there was a way.

Piper shook her head and met his eyes with an intensity that seemed to say there was nothing to do.

Still, Judah wished he knew some way to make the situation better or what to suggest, but he wasn't familiar with this kind of boat, and even if he was, he had a feeling it wasn't a fix one could easily do on the fly. Piper's expression had confirmed that.

He also had the feeling this hadn't just happened by accident. They'd walked away from the boat, taken for granted that no one was following them today.

Judah had forgotten, somehow, that whoever was after Piper wasn't indiscriminately shooting at her. Instead, they seemed to be trying to make her death look like an accident.

Just like they'd made several other deaths or near deaths look like accidents.

It felt, Judah realized as they hit another rapid and he lost his balance, more like a professional killer who was used to cleaning up messes and hiding them.

It was the last thought he had before he went underwater.

The icy water sucked the air from Judah's lungs as soon as he hit it. He'd never understood how that worked, but it took so much energy out of a person that even a good swimmer was rendered relatively hopeless after being submerged for a little while.

His head dipped as the current pulled him and Judah kicked his legs to give himself more flotation. Piper! Where was Piper? She was a strong swimmer but was already bruised from the recent attack against her, already worn out. What if she needed his help? He looked around for her, feeling water spray off his hair as he did so. The boat was farther downstream than he'd have expected.

Was she still on it? Could she be?

Judah didn't have long in, he knew. He had to get out. Hadn't they just talked about how this river meant almost certain death if someone fell in it? Well, there was a key word to that. *Almost.* His police training had provided some survival skills, too.

Still, he had never had training specific to this situation. Really, he was flying blind, but Judah didn't like that. He needed to feel confident, like the odds were not stacked against him.

He swam hard with his legs, and the current pulled him forward. He kicked sideways, toward the shore.

Painfully little progress that way.

Judah fought hard against the current, aimed for shore as he passed a limb and reached for it. He missed, his hands empty, falling face-first into the water. The sound of the splash was swallowed up by the raging current. This wasn't working. Maybe panic made you immediately exhaust yourself trying to get out.

He couldn't fight the current, that much was becoming clear. So working with it was his best option.

And Piper?

"Judah!" He heard a shout.

There, not as far downriver as he was. They must have fallen off at the same time. Why was she so far behind?

She could have gotten stuck on the rocks underneath and only just now made it up. That was a terrifying thought.

"Diagonal!" she yelled. At least, that was what he heard.

Judah frowned at her.

"Swim diagonal!"

Of course. He should have realized that. Judah did his best to relax, to gather strength. Then he took a deep breath, angling himself toward the shore at a diagonal, as Piper had said. As he swam, he prayed that Piper was okay. Everything in him wanted to rescue her, but the truth was that he'd probably drown them both if he tried. This was one of her strengths. This time taking care of her meant letting her handle herself, not trying to act like he could do better.

Help her get out, God. Helps us both get out.

Judah's hands barely caught on the edge of the riverbank, but he couldn't get a grip. Rocks, including the one he tried to grab, loosened from the shore and fell into the river, and slid back in the water. Another deep breath. More kicking.

He grabbed at the shore again. This time his hands burned from the friction against the rock, the way the jagged corners dug into his skin, but he didn't let go.

The river didn't take him.

He held on for another few seconds, not daring to rest longer, then took a deep breath and pulled himself out.

He was on the ground. He'd made it. Judah rolled over, sat up and looked back at the river, looking for Piper.

But he couldn't see her.

Not anywhere.

ELEVEN

Piper realized she never should have made that mistake. She had seen that Judah was close to the south edge of the river, on their left, as they were swept downstream. Rather than swim to her side, she'd tried to head for his so they wouldn't be separated.

Now she was running out of energy. Her mind had started to detach herself from the situation a little, to assess it scientifically. She would soon start to slip underwater. Then the rule of threes started to kick in. Three minutes without oxygen.

She needed so much more than three more minutes to live. She had things to do with her life, people to save.

A man to spend time with, decide if these feelings she had for him were the permanent, lasting kind.

Piper just could not die.

Had the boat breaking been an accident? It seemed impossible. The SAR team couldn't afford for the gear to be less than fully functional, so care was taken to service it properly and double-check—no, *triple*-check—everything that could possibly go wrong.

Piper had just done a pre-trip safety check before

they'd been out today, which meant…someone was trying to kill her. Again. Still. Why had she left the boat unattended earlier when they'd walked around to investigate the area where Nichole Richards had disappeared? It hadn't crossed her mind that someone could tamper with their transportation. And if they broke something on the fan, it wouldn't matter when it broke, just that it did. Then they'd be helpless in the water.

That was how Piper felt right now. Helpless.

Hopeless.

Like this was it.

She felt her chest tightening from the cold and the exhaustion, and reminded herself that right now she was okay. This was her body's natural response to the water temperature.

She'd made it to the left-hand side of the river, but her arms were so exhausted from the swim that she was having trouble getting a good grip on the riverbank's rocky edges. One more good try. She'd put everything she had into this one and hope for the best.

And pray that if it didn't work, then something else would happen.

"Piper!" She heard Judah shout but couldn't find him. She couldn't afford to use the energy it would take to look around. Instead she took a slow deep breath in, then reached for the shore.

Her hands caught the rocks. Started to slip.

Hands clamped down on top of hers as Judah fell to the ground at the edge of the river. "I've got you." He said, his voice steady. "And I'm not letting go."

Piper let him pull her out of the water and collapsed on the ground beside him. Tears were streaming down her face, mixing with the brackish water of the tidal river.

They were running out of time to find out who was after her. Because Piper didn't know how many more of these attempts she could survive.

It already felt like they were pushing their luck.

The next time might just be the one they couldn't escape.

She cried there for a few minutes, her body exhausted, her mind grieving the normal life she'd had before all of this. She'd also lost the boat. The team needed that.

"I've got to call Jake," she said around her sobs. "He might be able to get the boat if they head out soon and catch it."

Piper knew some people rafted on this river. While she personally thought it was ridiculously dangerous, it was possible they might be able to recover the boat with a raft. Well, if the fan had gone off.

She didn't know how that was possible. And she didn't have the brainpower to try to work it out right now, either. Piper pulled out her phone, filled Jake in. He promised to go look for the boat.

"Hey, it's going to be okay." Judah's voice should have been comforting, but it wasn't. Not this time. Piper was past being able to be comforted. This had gone on for too long.

"I can't do this anymore," she heard herself say and felt his arms wrap around her.

She'd never realized exactly how it would feel to be held by a man like Judah, someone who was more interested in giving than taking, someone who wanted the best for her. She struggled to even put words to the feeling, but *protected* came close.

Almost even *loved*. But it was too soon for words like that, and Judah might not feel that way about her. She wasn't meaning to assume anything about how he felt.

But it was how it made her feel.

"Let's get back to the police station."

"I want to go home." Her voice was small, and she hated it, but Piper had nothing left. She'd been pulling on reserves for so long that those were depleted. She needed…well, she didn't know exactly what, but not this.

"As soon as we give a statement, I'll take you right to Adriana and Levi's."

Home. She'd meant *her* home.

"Back there?" She didn't mean to be ungrateful. They'd both been great, but it just wasn't home; it wasn't normal.

"Piper, come on." Judah stood up, took her hand and helped her up, too. Then he took her other hand in his and turned her to face him. They stood there, both still dripping wet, and Piper leaned her head forward until her forehead rested on Judah's chest. She felt the rhythm of his breathing, constant and comforting, heard the beating of his heart.

He was so strong. So dependable.

She could so easily lose her heart to this man.

"I miss home." Had she only been gone for a day? She missed more than the building. She missed her routine, her job, everything about her life as it had been before this threat had interrupted it.

"I get it. I really do. And if you give me a list of things you want, I'll have an officer pack a bag for you and bring it to Adriana and Levi's, so it will be waiting when we get there."

Piper nodded slowly and looked away.

"Hey." Judah's voice was soft. Piper looked back at him.

Gentle hands tilted her chin up so that she was looking at him and her eyes met his. Judah's eyes searched her own.

"I understand you want normal right now. But it's not an option. Even if I sent you back home and we pretended everything was okay, it wouldn't be. We would be taking unnecessary risks because the danger is still out there. Someone needs you out of their way, Piper, and they aren't done yet. They aren't going to stop until you are out of the picture, do you understand?"

How could she so desperately want to be alive, while at the same time, someone desperately wanted her dead? It hurt to put it into words, to make herself acknowledge the fact that someone didn't want to "hurt" her or "scare" her.

Someone wanted to kill her. Forever.

She blew out a breath. "Levi and Adriana's as soon as we are done with the police station?"

"Yes."

"And you'll buy me pizza for dinner?"

"I'll buy you pizza for dinner." He had the hint of a smile in his voice.

It was enough, for now, to give Piper the strength she

needed to head down the river, along a narrow moose trail that wound along beside it, back toward town.

Judah had called in to the police department, letting them know what had happened. They'd promised to send an officer out to the scene. He hadn't anticipated it would be his brother. This reminded him all too much of when someone had been after Levi. Mixing family and police work was tricky enough anyway, but when one of them was in danger that felt personal?

It made it even more complicated.

"Be careful," Judah told Levi when they met on the trail. "The boat would have been tampered with about half a mile back up the river. Piper was showing me a scene of one of the recoveries she worked."

"And you think someone tampered with it?"

Judah hadn't given a lot of details over the phone, but filled his brother in now. Levi nodded, his face more serious than it ever was.

"What is going on here? This feels…" He shook his head.

"How does it feel to you?" Judah pressed. "Because I have my theories, but I don't know if I'm so close to it I'm not seeing something, or if I'm making connections that aren't really there."

"I mean, it's not going very well for them right now, but it feels almost like some kind of cleanup operation. They were eliminating people who had gotten in the way of something, and now Piper keeps stumbling upon them. Either they are worried she witnessed something she shouldn't have, or they're just tired of her rescuing their victims. And now she's a target, too."

"Cleanup is a good way to describe it." Judah looked over at Piper, who was listening wide-eyed. Of course she couldn't leave the two of them alone to talk when there was an active threat against her, and Judah wouldn't want her to, but truthfully he'd forgotten briefly that she was standing right there.

"Wait." Judah watched the expression on her face shift.

"You mean, like a hit man?"

Judah and Levi looked at each other. Judah looked back at Piper.

"We don't know yet."

She shivered. "Let's get out of here. Please."

Judah nodded at his brother and put his arm around Piper, helped her hurry down the trail.

"I hate what this is stealing from me. I love that river. I love that boat. I love my job. I don't want to be afraid to help people."

She sounded so torn, so upset that Judah wished he could fix it all, but he knew he couldn't.

"You can do this," he said instead, which felt to him like an empty promise, even though he meant every word. But what else was there to say?

He could do the interviews he wanted to do by himself. That was an option. But Judah had the feeling that really what she wanted was her life back. Since that wasn't an option, he really felt like she'd want to be involved.

But then again, wasn't that making a decision for her? Perhaps he should talk to her and give her the option to bow out, in case he was reading her or the situation wrong. After the way she had been abused and manipulated before, Judah wanted to make sure he didn't do anything to make her feel like she wasn't the one in charge of her own life.

"You're lost in thought," she finally said, but after quite some time, which made him think that she had been lost in thought, also.

"There's a lot to think about," he said truthfully.

She nodded.

When they reached the car, they climbed in silently and Judah drove to the police station. This was starting to feel almost routine, and not in a good way. He needed to do whatever it took to figure out who was behind the attacks.

But there were still so many pieces he wasn't connecting.

He thought about them, sitting beside Piper while she gave her statement.

First, Piper rescued a lot of people. They'd found three cases where the deaths or near deaths looked suspicious. So, say someone was killing those people and Piper was interrupting the murderer. Then Judah would have uncovered a motive for someone trying to kill Piper.

Even thinking that phrase hurt him. The idea that someone wanted Piper gone was heart-wrenching.

He cared about her. She was his friend, so it made sense. At least, that was what he tried to tell himself.

If his and Levi's instincts were right, a cleanup man, a hit man of sorts, did make sense. Someone hired him to make the messes go away. In a town as small as Raven Pass, a rash of shootings would have practically shut the place down. That would be an ineffective way to commit a string of crimes without being caught. Instead, to kill people in ways that looked natural, that made it seem like the wilderness was claiming another victim…

Well, it was brilliant in a thoroughly evil kind of way.

But who would pay to have people killed? Who would need messes cleaned up in Raven Pass?

They were a small town, located off the Seward Highway near Girdwood. They got their fair share of crime; sometimes drug trade from Anchorage spilled over, things like that. But multiple murders that seemed connected?

Judah didn't know where to start.

Piper was looking at him, and Judah realized she and the chief were done talking.

"Sorry, lost in thought."

"I'm sure the two of you want to get dried off and cleaned up." Chief Moore stood. "I'll let you go for now and get in touch if we have any more questions. Wicks, I'll have another officer cover for you the rest of your shift."

"Are you sure?" The chief was a fair man, a good boss, but Judah didn't want him making exceptions.

The chief's eyes went to Piper, then Judah. He nodded decisively. "I'm sure. Consider making sure no one gets close to her your job for the rest of the day."

That he could do. Judah nodded. "Yes, sir." And they went to the car and headed straight for his brother's house. No one was home, so Piper dried off and cleaned up in the guest room while Judah borrowed a change of clothes from his brother. They weren't quite the same size. The pants were a little long, the shirt a little snug in the arms and shoulders, but close enough.

Judah had grabbed the files from the police department on the search and rescue cases. They had a small file on each of them and Judah had earlier printed out the digital records and stuck them into manila envelopes to take them home.

"What's all that?"

"The case files. I don't have much, since the incidents weren't determined to be criminal at the time. But it's something."

Piper nodded, then walked over to sit beside him on the couch.

Her nearness was distracting, but that wasn't necessarily something he wanted her to know, the huge effect she had on him, so he said nothing. Instead he read down the list, focused on the observations the police had made.

After reading all three, he came to the same conclusion for all of them. The police hadn't been wrong not to pursue any of them. But he could definitely see some holes in the stories, enough that in retrospect he could see that they should have been investigated more thoroughly.

Also, he really needed to talk to the other people who had been involved.

"I've got a question for you," he said to Piper.

She looked over at him. "What's up?"

"I need to interview some of the attempted victims if they're still alive, maybe some other people who were associated with these cases. The biggest gap we have in the investigation right now is that we don't know why someone was targeting all these people. If there's no connection, it could be a serial killer. But I agree with Levi. I think some kind of hit man is more likely what we are looking at, which means there has to be a link between them. Someone is getting rid of some people for a certain reason."

"Okay, so what do you need from me?"

"Well, it depends." He looked at her. Waited. "Do you want to be involved, or would you rather not?"

"What do you mean?" She frowned. "You want to know if I'm out? Is that it?"

"It's not your job, Piper. And I've asked a lot of you. Today was awful, not knowing if you'd make it out of the river. Really not knowing if either of us would. I don't want to go through that again. But I don't want to refuse your help if you're offering." He rubbed a hand on his forehead. "I don't know what's better anymore, for you to help or not help. I'm doing my best to keep you safe either way and it's still not enough. So at this point I just want to know what you want."

Instead of replying right away, Piper said nothing, but she did nod, and she looked like she was considering everything he'd said.

"If I keep helping…" She trailed off. "I'm not in the way, right?"

"Not at all," he told her truthfully. Yes, she was distracting, but she'd be that even if she wasn't with him.

Piper nodded. "I want to help, still." She smiled. "Thank you for letting me pick."

So he'd been correct about that one. Judah was deeply relieved he hadn't offended her. Instead it actually seemed like he'd done the right thing. "You're welcome. How do you feel about seeing if anyone is available to talk to us today?"

She winced. "I guess there's no reason to delay."

"The sooner we get all this figured out, the better off you'll be. Safer."

"I know." Her expression still didn't seem certain. "I get all of that. I'm just so tired. Let me go grab shoes."

Judah knew she wanted to help, but he also believed her that she was tired. She had dark circles under her eyes that hadn't been there a few days ago. The case was taking a toll on all of them, but especially on Piper. He wanted to stick to his decision and let her help, but that might take some effort. He was a protector. He also wanted to be able to tell her to step back, take a rest.

Maybe instead he'd have to arrange some rest for both of them.

"Got my shoes. Let's go." They walked to the car together, Judah's mind already working on how he could give them both a little bit of a break the next day.

TWELVE

The first house they pulled up to belonged to Randy Walcott, who had almost drowned after operating a canoe while intoxicated. He had almost nothing useful to tell them, since he couldn't remember the accident at all due to how much alcohol he had consumed. They'd asked him about that and he'd admitted he'd just had too much to drink and not enough food. There was no reason to suspect his drink had been spiked, since he'd been alone.

"Do you know why someone might be after you?" Judah asked.

The man shook his head. "No. You think someone still is?" He seemed to consider this, then nodded. "I can see that."

The words made Judah frown. "You still feel like you're in danger?"

He frowned. "I don't know that I'd say that, but..." He trailed off. "Actually I would, yes. Several times since the accident, I've felt like someone is following me. I don't know that I have enough solid evidence of that to be helpful to you guys, but it's a hunch I've had anyway."

It wouldn't hold up in court, but it was enough for Judah to take notice and pay attention.

"Thanks for talking to us today," Judah said as he and Piper moved from his front deck back toward the truck. "Call if anything else comes to mind."

He nodded. "I'll do that. And I hope you guys figure out whatever it is you're working on."

"Thanks, we appreciate it," Piper said with a smile.

They got back into the car and Judah pulled out of the driveway. "That could have been more helpful."

"You had to know he wouldn't remember much, considering how intoxicated he'd been." Piper said.

"Yeah, but I thought we'd be able to get a better picture of who could be after him. I believe him that he feels like he's being watched, and that would make sense. But by who?"

Next they drove to the address listed for the man Piper had rescued from the rock ledge. It was an apartment building. As they climbed from the car, Judah tried to keep his level of awareness high. It would be easy for someone to follow them and try to take a shot at Piper.

It was a way that you couldn't live for very long before it started to weigh on you. Judah knew that he was exhausting himself. But what else could he do?

They walked to the door and Judah reached his hand up to knock.

A woman answered the door. Probably early forties, maybe late thirties. She looked tired. Her blondish hair was pulled into a messy bun and she didn't look pleased to have visitors.

"Is Jay Jones home?" Judah asked. "I'm from Raven

Pass PD. We'd like to talk to him, ask him about an accident he was involved in several months back."

The woman frowned. "Sorry, no one by that name lives here."

Judah felt Piper's gaze on him and glanced in her direction. She looked afraid. There was no other way to say that.

And for good reason, possibly.

"Okay, thank you."

The woman shut the door before he'd even finished talking.

Then she eased it open again. Judah's shoulders immediately tensed. He couldn't think of any good explanation for why she would be opening the door again, especially after the chilly reception she had given them the first time.

"Look." She blew out a breath and shook her head. "I don't like it when people come around asking about him, okay? Yeah, he lived here before, right up until he moved to Anchorage. I rented the place not long after. Never met the guy. I didn't know anything about him until the first person came here wanting to talk about him and said he'd lived here, and I looked him up online and found out he got killed in Anchorage sometime in the last week or so. No, I don't know anything about it, I don't want any trouble and I don't want to talk about it anymore, okay? But I guess it's not your fault so many other people have come by asking for him, so I'm sorry if I was a little ruder than necessary."

"He was killed?" Piper asked before Judah could stop her.

"You didn't know? Oh..." She looked back and forth

between the two of them like she was trying to figure out the nature of their relationship. "Were you and Jay..." she asked Piper. "Did you know him well?"

"Not at all, actually, but we had some things in common and I'd hoped to talk to him." Piper's expression darkened and it felt to Judah like the full realization of what had happened to the man they had hoped to talk to was sinking in. "I'm sorry to hear about his death."

"Me, too. Wish I'd never heard about it. Maybe soon I'll get a new place so people quit asking me. Might have been easier, you know, if he hadn't known so many people. But apparently he had a lot of friends." She lowered her voice. "And at least one enemy."

"We've got to be going." Judah said. "Thank you for talking to us, and I hope people stop asking you about him."

"I certainly do, too. You two take care." She shut the door again, this time slowly, but firmly. It did not open again.

"Huh." Piper breathed out. "So someone killed him."

"It makes our theory look even more possible. Especially when you consider the fact that Randy said someone was following him also."

"He *thinks* someone is following him and he *feels* like he's being watched," Piper pointed out.

Judah was already shaking his head. "Sure, but it's still a legitimate concern on his part. Given even more legitimacy by what we just found out."

"Can we call him and warn him, or something? I don't feel good about just leaving him out there. If they meant for him to be dead, it seems only logical that they're going to continue to come after him until they've killed him, too."

"Get in the car first." Judah was worried about the guy, as well, but not as much as he was worried about Piper. First he needed her out of harm's way, at least as much as he was able to get her right now, and then he could worry about the other people affected by this news, and start to think through what it meant.

Everything fit too well together to be coincidence, and Judah didn't believe in coincidences anyway.

They drove back to the police department. On the way there, Judah called Randy, who promised to be careful and said he appreciated the warning.

Then he called a friend of his in Anchorage at the police department there to confirm that Jay had been killed. They didn't have any leads yet on who was responsible, as it was a relatively recent murder—recent enough to have been in the Anchorage newspaper for a few days, his friend said. That explained how the woman who now lived in Jay Jones's apartment had known about his murder, but it was recent enough that it was a current case and his friend couldn't give him many details. Judah would need to remember to call back later and find out more.

But it looked like a murder. He had bruising consistent with a struggle.

Whoever was responsible for cleaning up the loose ends in whatever this mess was, he was thorough. And that made Judah even more determined to solve this. Because it meant no matter how many attempts there had been on Piper's life, and how many times she got away unscathed, whoever was after her wasn't going to quit. This was going to be a constant battle day after day, to maintain their vigilance while not overwhelming her with the truth of the restrictions she needed to be under for her own safety.

It was a tightrope, one Judah felt he was already failing to walk. The faster they had a name of someone behind this, a motive, and could wrap it up, the better.

"So, what now?" Piper asked.

Judah had planned to interview several friends of the woman who had died and told Piper as much. "But I don't want to do it now. I'm uncomfortable knowing our talking to them could put a target on their backs. If someone is cleaning up messes, I don't want to make any more messes for them to clean, if you get what I'm saying."

Piper nodded, her eyes saying she got it. Judah wished he could fix the soul-deep fatigue he saw in her eyes.

Then again...

Maybe he could?

He wasn't sure yet what the next step in the investigation should be. It would come to him; he'd probably just bring work home with him tonight and sit up until all hours thinking through everything, like he'd been doing for the past few days.

But if he worked some more tonight, he could take the morning off. Piper had once been his favorite person to climb with.

Could he ask her to be his partner again? And would she appreciate the chance to take a break from the case?

Judah knew a place they could climb where the threat against her would be fairly nonexistent. It was an hour's drive back into the depths of the Chugach Range, but the climbing there was fantastic, and it was above the tree line, so the line of sight went on forever. No one would be able to approach without detection. All that combined, he was comfortable with the amount of risk it would add.

Especially when you considered how much reward potential it had. Piper couldn't continue this pace much longer. She was a strong woman, he knew, but even strong people had their breaking points. The last thing he wanted was to push Piper past hers.

"I have an idea for tomorrow."

She waited, watching him.

"What would think about going climbing with me?"

"A day off from the case?" she asked, sitting up a little straighter in the car seat.

Judah laughed. "Yeah, what do you say?"

"I think it sounds fantastic."

He loved hearing that enthusiastic tone from her, loved her zeal for life.

Judah nodded. "It's settled, then. That's what we'll do." But instead of feeling completely relaxed and optimistic, he still felt a sense of foreboding he couldn't quite shake. Piper needed this time. He was confident of that. Judah could only pray he wasn't making a huge mistake.

For the first time in days, Piper woke up without the feeling of pressing exhaustion weighing her down. Just for this morning she was going to do her best to forget everything that was going on in her life and simply be present in the moment. Climbing with Judah again...

It had been almost a year. They'd danced together on the rocks back then; that was the only way Piper knew how to explain how well they had climbed together.

Getting ready proved to be something of a challenge. Judah had swung her by her house the night before to pick up some climbing clothes and her gear and then brought her back to his brother and sister-in-law's house, so that wasn't it. It was more the question of how she looked in general.

Did she go without makeup, like she usually did when climbing? Or look a little more put together, like she would if this was a date?

It wasn't a date. She knew that much. Judah had only suggested it because he knew she needed a break, Piper was fairly certain. But she wasn't going to overlook the gift that it was.

Still, mascara never hurt.

She finished getting ready and then walked out into the living room. Adriana whistled.

"What? I'm going climbing." Piper shrugged.

"With Judah, I'm assuming?"

"Why?"

"Because I know he wouldn't let you go off on your own. And it doesn't seem like the kind of activity you would try to do alone right now, so it seemed like a good guess."

"It was," Piper admitted.

"Hey." Adriana smiled. "I'm sorry, I shouldn't tease you. The truth is that I want both of you happy. And if this makes you both happy…"

"I don't know if it does."

"You haven't talked about it?"

Piper shook her head.

"Well, talk to him. What could it hurt?"

That was the question that kept echoing in Piper's mind after Judah picked her up and they started driving to the crag. *What could it hurt?*

Taking the chance didn't feel worth the risk to her.

Deeply ironic for someone who enjoyed a hobby that was so much about taking calculated risks.

The sun was bright in the sky when they pulled up to Anchor Rock.

"Gorgeous day to climb."

Judah nodded. "It is. And I think you could use the break."

"Just me, huh?" Piper teased, opening her trunk and pulling carabiners and Camalots out and clipping them to the place on her harness. She hadn't climbed here in a while and didn't remember exactly what piece of protection she needed to be prepared to place, so she put most of her rack on, knowing it was better to have too many than not enough. She checked all of her gear even more thoroughly than usual, just in case someone could have sabotaged it. Everything looked good.

"Okay, both of us could." He grinned at her. Wow, she could get used to seeing him smile that way.

It reminded her of the face he'd shown her the night they first met. She'd been climbing here alone, and Judah had asked if she wanted a belay partner. She'd made some comment, half teasing, Piper didn't even remember what she'd said now, and he'd grinned like that. Then she'd tied herself into his rope so he could belay her, and she'd wondered if she was doing the right thing, putting her life in the hands of someone she barely knew.

It turned out to be one of the most exhilarating things she'd ever done. Judah was a good belayer. She'd climbed with people before who kept too much tension on the rope, which could interfere with a climber's movements, but she'd also climbed with people who left so much slack in it that Piper had wondered why she bothered with the rope at all. Judah kept a perfect balance and she felt his attention on her the entire time she was climbing. That was probably why she'd sent her first 5.11, because he'd been watching.

She hadn't climbed as much since he'd disappeared from her life. Once she'd known what it was like to climb with a partner like that, it made it harder to settle for just anyone.

Maybe that was what she was afraid of now. She'd been kissed before Judah, but never like that, never in a way that he'd made her feel. She'd known the night before last that he cared about her much more than he was willing to admit; it was a kiss that had been given to her, not one he'd taken from her. Piper didn't know if she'd be able to articulate the difference if someone had asked, but she could feel it. Not that anyone was going to ask, because Piper certainly wasn't going to be talking about it. She was somewhat surprised Adriana hadn't asked straight out if they'd kissed, but her teammate had been uncharacteristically gentle with her questioning about Judah.

Piper appreciated that. The entire relationship felt like a soap bubble. Shiny and exciting and beautiful but something that might break if it was handled too roughly.

She didn't want it to burst.

"Which route first?" Judah asked her.

"Secret Santa is one of my favorites." She mentioned one of the best 5.11s on the wall.

"Let's do that one, then. You climb first?"

Piper smiled her thanks. Then she tied her rope onto her harness, double-checking to make sure all the loops were operating the way they were supposed to.

"On belay?" she asked, even though she'd been climbing for years and not everyone went through the ritual once they had more experience. As a search and rescue worker, though, Piper knew better than to assume that because she'd done something many times that it made the activity safe. It was better to mitigate risks where she could; that way she felt better about the ones she did take.

"Belay on," Judah replied.

"Climbing."

"Climb on."

Piper reached up, found the first hold easily with her right hand and pressed her left hand out against a slight protrusion in the rock. This route was one of her favorites because of how much it depended on footwork. Piper had decent upper body strength, but routes like this, with small crimps for the hands, which required an artistic, gymnastic sort of movement to get through, were her favorite.

Judah preferred routes with big moves, where he had to jump for the next hold, almost like he should have been a boulderer. Which was funny, because he wasn't the kind of guy she pictured as liking big risks. Apparently climbing was the only part of his life where he let that side of himself come out.

Piper continued up the wall, pausing at the crux to remember how she'd gotten through this most difficult part of the route before. Left hand there…step up with the right foot, right hand up, switch the feet…

She moved through the rest of the route seamlessly, sent it—climber-speak for successfully ascending a route—and then rappelled back down.

"Nice job." The approval shining in Judah's eyes made her feel good. Piper grinned. "Your turn."

Judah started climbing, and she held the rope, pulling it when necessary, her hands burning from the friction against her skin.

He made it to the top also, though not quite as easily as Piper had. He slipped in one section and Piper paid close attention, thinking he was going to come off the wall, but he caught himself and kept going.

After he rappelled down, he laughed. "Not quite as clean a send as yours."

Piper shrugged. "Yeah, but you and I both know I picked this climb because it's one of the ones I'm best at."

"And here I thought it was just coincidence, not that you wanted to show off."

"Did I say show off?" She was surprised at how easy it was to flirt with him, still. "I wasn't trying to show off."

"You didn't have to try."

And then Piper was standing closer to him than she

meant to be. He was still tied into the harness, the rope held loosely in her hands.

"Did you…" She swallowed hard. "Did you want to climb this one again? Or go do another line?"

"If that's what you want."

"We should," she said without knowing why. Because she wanted to climb with him more and not have this day end? Or because she was afraid of what another kiss with Judah would do to her?

Not that he would hurt her intentionally. Judah wasn't that kind of man. It was more of the fact that Piper was afraid that if she kissed him again, she would lose her heart so completely that she would never get it back. And Judah hadn't done or said anything to make her sure that he'd changed his mind about wanting to be in a relationship.

That was the problem with middle-of-the-night kisses that weren't followed by some kind of relationship-defining conversation.

"Let's climb Veins of Gold," Piper suggested just to change the subject.

Judah looked at her. Frowned.

Then looked farther up the pass. Toward…

Gray Mountain Mine. The local gold mine had been the subject of a lot of controversy with environmental groups and Raven Pass citizens alike. Some people were in favor, since it brought jobs to the area, but most were opposed. Big gold mining operations could be harmful to the environment.

"Actually, can we take a rain check on the rest of our climbing day? I think we have to get back to the case."

"Now?" Piper blinked a few times, but nodded.

"We need to go ask the people at Gray Mountain Mine some questions," Judah said, his tone resolute.

"You think the mine has something to do with the murders?"

Judah hesitated. "Call it a hunch."

Piper'd had the same one when he'd looked in the direction of the mine. She wished they hadn't lost the rest of their relaxing day together, but she understood. The case had to come first. Was it because she was involved or would work always come first with Judah? How would it be to date someone whose job was so pressing that workaholism was encouraged?

She didn't know. But she didn't have any more time to think about it now. They had people to talk to. A case to solve.

THIRTEEN

Still dressed in their climbing clothes, Judah and Piper headed for Gray Mountain Mine.

"What exactly are you going to ask them?" Piper wondered from beside him. "And why? We don't even know if there are any connections to the people who were killed."

"I'm still working on that," Judah admitted. "But I didn't think until just now when you mentioned the route with gold in the name. When we went by Randy Walcott's house, I saw a Gray Mountain logo on the hat he was wearing. Pull up their website and see if you find him listed anywhere."

"I doubt they have all three hundred employees listed," Piper said.

"Good point. Look it up anyway, if you will, and tell me who the workers listed are. I want to go into this knowing what I'm looking for."

"Which is?" In his peripheral vision he could see her doing what he'd asked, though.

"Someone in management at the mine who might want to kill people."

"Kill them why?"

"Have you read the paper lately? For the last twelve to eighteen months it's been article after article about the changes Gray Mountain has made and how it's less environmentally friendly than they promised the town of Raven Pass they would be when they built the mine. The public is losing confidence in them. I just read something recently. What if someone tried to kill an employee to make a statement, convince the mine it wasn't worth operating here?"

"What about the other murders?"

Judah shook his head. Then frowned. "Maybe it's the opposite, then. Maybe someone from the mine is killing people who oppose them."

Those words hung in the silence and Piper shivered, then continued with the online research Judah had asked her to do.

"Okay, your top guy is Malcom Everett. Other names listed online are Lisa Harlow and Mike Turner."

"Thanks." Judah turned into the entrance to the mine office and hoped someone would be willing to answer his questions. Next to him, Piper was still on her phone, though he wasn't sure what she was doing. He pulled into a parking spot and was looking around at the campus, when Piper spoke in a voice that made him still.

"Wait, here's Randy Walcott's LinkedIn profile. He works there, too."

Judah nodded. Piper tapped away at her phone and then breathed in sharply.

"Judah."

Her voice was soft and urgent, and immediately brought him to attention.

"I looked at the *Raven Pass Gazette* online to see the articles you mentioned. One of the journalists who wrote all those articles about the mine?"

"Yeah?"

"It was Nichole. The woman who died in the river after allegedly falling in while she was camping."

He looked over at Piper, not able to stop the excitement in his expression. He could feel it. "We're close, Piper. It's not a coincidence that two of the three victims or near victims were tied to the mine."

"I wonder if there's a connection with the man who was just killed in Anchorage, Jay Jones. The hiker I saved who was killed."

"I would be confident in saying there must be. We'll figure it out, but for now, I think we're getting close. Let's go figure out what the mine stands to lose and who could be involved."

"If they'll let us talk to them."

Piper's words were as unoptimistic as her tone, and for good reason. Their reception from the administrative assistant was nothing short of chilly. The top guy wouldn't see them, but Lisa Harlow, the assistant manager of the mine, agreed to talk to them.

"She can give you five minutes," the admin said, a slight, patronizing smile on her face. "But she's very busy."

"Thank you, we appreciate it," Judah said. They were led to a small office where they waited. A woman whom Judah guessed to be in her forties walked in.

"Hello, I'm Lisa Harlow." She shook both of their hands. Her handshake was tighter than it needed to be.

Judah found that interesting; it tended to imply that someone had something to prove.

"I'm Officer Wicks, with Raven Pass Police Department. This is Piper McAdams. She's assisting me on a case."

He felt Piper smile at him.

"I don't know what the police would need to do here. We're current on our inspections and we pride ourselves on being a positive contribution to the community," Lisa said forcefully.

Piper spoke up before he could stop her. "I suppose that's why the community is pushing back against your proposed expansion and the newspaper is running articles about the heavy metals your mine seems to be leaching back into the soil in the community. That's the positive contribution?"

He shot her a look. Obviously it didn't take much work to figure out which side of the hotly debated Gray Mountain Mine issue she was on. But this was bigger than the politics currently dividing their little town.

"Not everyone will agree with what we are doing here, but we have documentation that we are doing a fantastic job of being cognizant of important environmental issues."

Lisa's expression had wavered, though. Piper's words, though they might have been delivered hastily and a bit unwisely, had hit home. And it was possible she might have saved Judah some time and effort because they were already talking about the issues that seemed to factor into the case.

"On that subject, out of curiosity, is there any kind of complaint handling system? I know the mine does en-

deavor to be sustainable and environmentally friendly."
Judah tried to put things as gently as he could so they
didn't completely alienate one of the people who might
be able to help them.

"There isn't a reason for people to complain," she
insisted.

Piper just stared at her, her expression blank and un-
impressed. Judah almost laughed, but he stayed quiet.

The woman blew out a breath. "Yes, we have a complaint form on our website. Believe me, most of them
are ridiculous. Someone will accuse us of making too
much noise, when we are all tucked back into the woods
here, with no houses within half a mile. Some people
just like to complain."

"Do you have a record of people who have made
complaints?" Judah asked, keeping himself going down
the same track. It had occurred to him just a little while
ago that the people being targeted could have been com-
plaining about the mine in some capacity. While that
alone didn't seem like reason enough to kill, it could
be tied to something else.

He felt like he was taking investigative stabs in the
dark, but he'd focused so much of his energy on Piper,
on keeping her safe, that he hadn't had a chance to do
as much research into connections between the victims
as he liked. He also felt more pressed for time than he
usually was. A ticking clock was one thing when he was
protecting a victim he didn't know. He still cared, still
worked hard and did his best, but there was no getting
around the fact that his feelings for Piper were making
him work this one differently. Right now he wasn't sure
if that was a good or a bad thing.

"I have a record," Lisa finally answered.

"We'd like to see it."

"Do you have a warrant?"

"Is there a reason we would need one?"

She stared at him. Shook her head. "I'll get them to you. Leave an email address with me and I will send them before I head home for the day."

It was the most they were going to get for now, Judah felt, so he nodded. "Thank you, we appreciate it." He walked toward the door. Piper followed.

They went back down the long hallway, their footsteps echoing all the way to the glass front doors.

"What did you think?" Piper asked when they'd stepped outside.

Judah shook his head. He wasn't ready to talk about it yet. Not at a place like this, which likely had them on some kind of closed-circuit TV right now.

They continued to the car, and when they were both inside, Judah turned to her.

"I think we're onto something," he said with a grin.

"I agree, but I don't know what the connection is, do you?" Piper asked. Judah just blinked and she shrugged. "It's not my job to figure these kinds of things out. Water rescue? Now, you probably won't find someone better at it."

He liked that she was confident about her strengths but didn't downplay her weaknesses. She knew she wasn't the best at everything but wasn't the type to profess a lot of false modesty, either.

Judah put the car in gear. "Let's get away from here. I don't like feeling watched." He drove back down the lane, past where they had climbed, and then pulled into a narrow road.

"Really?" Piper raised her eyebrows. "You're taking me to Lover's Ridge?"

"To talk," he insisted, feeling his cheeks start to heat up. And he wasn't a guy who did a lot of blushing. But it was true that he was taking Piper to a popular post-date spot that overlooked the river. They needed to be somewhere private to talk about what they'd learned and maybe research on their phones, but he hadn't wanted to go back to his brother's house. He needed a little more time alone with Piper first. Just talking to her was intoxicating, the way she captured his attention.

Even if what he should focus on right now was the case, he would rather do it with Piper beside him.

"I was teasing." Piper sounded embarrassed.

"Hey, I know." He smiled at her, hoping they were back on easy footing now, but it did feel more and more complicated to talk to her, ever since those kisses. What had it been, two days ago? It had been the most surreal experience, especially since neither of them had mentioned it and nothing had really changed between them...

Well, that wasn't true. Nothing had changed outwardly, except maybe he'd held her hand since then. Everything had changed inside, at least for him; he just didn't know how to talk to her about it, what to say. It was the worst timing ever for starting a relationship, and Judah still wasn't sure it was the wisest choice anyway. He wanted better for Piper than what he had to offer. He knew his faults and knew that he probably worked too hard.

Should he talk to her?

He wasn't good with words like that. He'd never been that guy.

Instead he just sat there, silence surrounding them, wondering if he was missing his chance.

"So, what did you want to talk about?" Piper asked to prompt him. Anything to end this awkward silence.

"The case." He frowned. "I don't think I'm reaching by thinking that Gray Mountain is involved somehow."

"More than one person at the mine, you mean?"

"Okay, I might have misstated that. I think someone there is involved and the mine might be part of what's going on that is getting people killed."

Piper nodded, processing what he'd said. "So the connection with Randy was that he works there, right?"

Judah nodded.

"And the woman who drowned was a journalist," she said slowly. "What about Jay, the man who was just killed?"

"I don't know." Judah frowned. "I called a friend at APD who confirmed that it looked like a murder, but he couldn't tell me any more at the moment. I forgot to follow up with him."

"Hey," Piper started to say. "Don't beat yourself up. It's been really busy lately. Overwhelmingly so."

"Mistakes get people killed in my job."

Piper glared at him long enough for him to have realization dawn on him. The same happened to her. "Oh…yeah…"

"Yeah, so I get it."

"Hey, but none of this is your fault." Judah shook

his head. "You've got to remember that. All these cases we are wading back into... I'm sure they take a toll emotionally. But you didn't make mistakes with these. Someone was intentionally killing people."

"I wish we knew who." Piper let out a sigh. The hardest thing about Judah's line of work, she'd decided, was that it was full of so many extremes. One second you were running from bullets, and everything was high stress, and then there was waiting, working, investigating. The waiting was almost worse.

"Oh." Judah's voice was serious.

"What?" Piper looked over at Judah, who had pulled out his phone to look at a text message.

"Jay was murdered, according to Anchorage Police. It happened just north of the city, on a trail near Eagle River. From what I'm reading, it looks like it was set up similar to the rescues you made. Made to look like an accident, someone called it in, but of course Jay was dead when help arrived."

"You think the same person killed him?" she asked.

Judah nodded.

"So whoever it is has specific targets..."

Judah finished. "All of whom have some kind of relation to the gold mine. My contact in Anchorage just clarified what Jay did for a living."

"What was it?"

Judah nodded. "He was a scientist who was responsible for some of the testing done near the mine site. The examinations revealed that they weren't taking the kind of environmental precautions they were supposed to be taking."

He started the car. "We should probably head back. You need to get some food and rest."

Judah realized his mistake before she had a chance to. "I mean, I want you to be able to rest if you want." He rubbed his forehead. "I don't want to tell you what to do, Piper. I just care about you. You can tell me when I'm doing that, okay?"

Something in her chest warmed. He cared about her enough to invite her to tell him when something bothered her. That felt like a big step to her, somehow.

The car was quiet as they drove back to town, neither of them speaking about the events of the day. Piper wanted to talk, but she wasn't sure Judah was in the mood for it. Even after they'd kissed, even after the fantastic time they'd had climbing today, she didn't know where she stood with Judah. Neither of them had talked about it and that was okay with Piper. It seemed less like an avoidance of commitment on either of their parts and more the way one would treat something fragile. You didn't try to catch a soap bubble unless you wanted it to pop.

Maybe it was a bad thing for her to be this uncertain of a relationship, this careful with it, after what she'd been through. Piper wasn't sure. But all she knew was that she cared enough about Judah that she didn't want anything to go wrong with this.

"You hungry?" he asked her, nodding toward Micky's Diner, on the side of the narrow highway.

It was a dive, but one that was supposed to have good french fries anyway. Piper would sacrifice a lot of nutritional value and culinary skill for a serving or two of really good fries.

"Starving," she answered and he pulled the car over. It was difficult to quantify, even to herself, exactly what had changed with their relationship today. It wasn't that they'd kissed; they hadn't. And that was something they'd done days ago. More than likely it was the fact that today had been an odd blend of old times, of climbing together and laughing, and they worked well together as investigators.

Piper climbed out and took Judah's hand when he offered it. He held it only long enough to help her out of the car and then released it.

They walked across the parking lot and Judah held the door for her.

The diner was one big room, with wood paneling that made it feel warm and dated.

"Two?" a waitress asked, and Piper nodded. They were led to a table in the back corner, one without any other people around, which was saying something because the place was actually fairly crowded. A dance floor sat in another corner, and several couples were out there, dancing to a country song popular twenty or so years ago. They sat down and Judah grabbed his menu. Piper did the same, thankful to hide behind it for a few minutes.

Had he decided that kissing her had been a mistake? Had it been a one-time thing born out of worry for her, and not something he had planned to act on?

But she'd thought maybe…

Two steps forward, one step back.

She let out a breath and focused on the menu. "Do

you know what you'd like?" the waitress asked when she came back.

Piper looked at Judah, took him all in. His warm brown eyes, the way he had laugh lines that crinkled up when he smiled. His grin that was sometimes unexpected but so sincere.

Yeah, she knew what she'd like, all right.

"I'll have the patty melt and fries," she answered once she was able to tear her eyes away from Judah.

"I'll have the same." He handed the menu off, and it was like he didn't want to break the eye contact, either.

They sat for minute in quiet before Judah spoke up. "While we wait...want to dance?"

Her heart might have skipped. Kisses were one thing, but the thought of being wrapped in his arms...

"Yes, I'd love to." She heard herself say it out loud, in a voice much calmer than how she felt.

He offered her his hand and led her to the floor. The song that had just come on was a slow one, from the 1990s, about a man who was tired of pretending he wasn't still in love with a woman.

Judah released her hand, wrapped his arms around her waist instead. His touch focused all of her senses, and she blinked up at him, wondering if this man had any idea how strong her feelings for him were. Her arms rested on his shoulders, then wrapped around his neck almost without hesitation.

He pulled her closer.

The song played in the background. Piper was fairly sure she saw the expression on Judah's face change at one point. Then she heard him singing quietly.

Her breath caught.

Was he only singing the song, or did he feel the same things in the song?

Piper didn't know. But she knew that when he pulled her even closer and she laid her head down on his shoulder, it was the most natural thing. However he felt, one thing was for sure.

She loved him.

She couldn't pretend she didn't anymore.

FOURTEEN

Piper's head was resting on his shoulder and, for a moment, Judah felt like everything was right with the world. The weight of his job and responsibilities didn't hang on his shoulders, and he wasn't afraid for her safety, though he wasn't letting his guard down, either. He just *was* right there in the moment, holding Piper, wishing he could hold her every day for the rest of his life.

The music played on and they continued dancing, Judah pulled her even closer, his arms tightening around her, and she didn't protest.

Her glacier-blue eyes looked up at him now, wide and innocent, rimmed by her dark eyelashes. She was looking at him like he was her hero and it made him want to prove her right. He would do anything to be who she saw him as.

His gaze lowered to her lips. He'd already kissed her, twice on that one night, but doing so now would bring up more questions. Conversations. Judah didn't know what to do. He'd been so sure he would just live out his life alone.

"I don't want to hurt you." He didn't mean to say the words out loud and didn't realize he had until she picked her head up off his shoulder, then looked up at him and blinked in confusion.

"What do you mean?"

"This…" He trailed off. Cleared his throat. "Piper, back then, before…I never really gave you a reason why I ended things."

"You didn't," she admitted. The song ended and another started, another slow one. They kept dancing, their movements growing more and more together, their bodies pulling closer toward each other like a force Judah couldn't fight and didn't want to.

"It was because of my brother."

"Levi?" Piper tilted her head. "Does he not like me, or…"

Her voice was hesitant, vulnerable, and Judah wanted to ask her how anyone could not like her, not love her. She was everything he'd never known he wanted in a woman. Gutsy and brave, beautiful, smart.

"He likes you. Everyone likes you, Piper."

He saw the words fall on her, relax her expression. If they had that much of an impact, Judah wanted to spend the rest of his life telling her things like that. Things that were true, that she might not believe, but that he wanted her to know.

"What do you mean, then?" she asked as they continued to dance. Maybe nothing had changed outwardly, maybe they looked the same as they had dancing a few minutes ago, but Judah could feel her pulling away from him, at least inside. He was doing this all wrong, as he'd known he would, but he didn't want to be. He wanted to do better.

But Piper deserved to know why he hadn't given them a chance. He owed her at least that much.

"My brother got divorced a while back, before he fell in love with Adriana. It was partially because of his job."

"He has the same job as you... Oh..." Piper nodded, her expression saying she was starting to put the pieces together. "You don't want to have a relationship that..."

"That gets torn apart because of a job I promised to do. It's a job that matters to me. I can't..." Was he really going to mess up his chances with Piper before things even got started? It felt like that was what honesty would do right now, but at the same time Piper was a woman to be honest with, not someone to dance around the truth with, finesse his way around the hard questions. Maybe that was why he had run in the first place. He could sense she wasn't like just any woman. She was important to him; she mattered, her opinion mattered. It was because of that that Judah knew he had to have this conversation. Maybe a dance floor in the middle of what could have been only a magical moment wasn't the place for it, but this was who he was. He was doing the best that he could. "I can't quit law enforcement, Piper. It's who I am."

"What are you talking about?"

"I can't quit."

"And having a relationship would mean you had to?"

"Having a good one." He stepped back, ran a hand through his hair in frustration. "That's what it looks like to me, Piper. I mean, I know no one is talking marriage here, except about what happened to my brother, but you know what I learned when Levi's fell apart? I did some research, trying to help him out, figure out what to say to him, and half of police marriages end in divorce. *Half.* I can't do that to a woman, not one I really care about."

"There are always two people in a relationship." Her voice was insistent. Firm.

The music in the background had changed to a faster song, but they weren't dancing anymore anyway. They were standing, on the verge of someone yelling and walking away. Judah could feel it. See, this was why he hadn't thought a relationship would be a good idea. Relationships took two people determined to work on them, to say yes to each other, to loving each other, no matter what happened or how hard it got. He could promise to hold up his end, and he knew someone like Piper would do the same—but nothing was guaranteed.

Maybe that was why he kept using what had happened to Levi as a shield to hide behind. Maybe the truth was more than just not wanting to hurt someone else… Maybe he was afraid to get hurt, too.

"Yeah, but there are two people. Things could… happen." His voice wavered, broke ever so slightly. He swallowed hard, squaring his shoulders against her reaction.

Instead of arguing with him like he'd expected, Piper stepped closer. Laid an arm on his shoulder.

"Of course you can't quit your job. It's part of who you are and you're good at it."

He met her eyes. Blinked.

Piper shook her head. "But it doesn't mean you have

to give up on relationships. The right woman would never ask you to quit your job." Her gaze didn't waver. "And she would never give up on you."

The music ended. There were a couple of seconds of silence. Piper stayed where she was, leaving the next move up to him.

As a slow song started, Judah stepped forward and reached out for Piper. She stepped toward him, hesitantly at first, then closer, till she was folded back into his arms.

Judah had never been in love before, really had never been close. He didn't know a lot about it, but he knew that it felt like Piper belonged there and everything inside him that had been tense had stilled. He felt something very much like peace.

Was this part of what love was, too? Having an argument and knowing you weren't really mad at the other person? To be able to know that sometimes two people just disagreed?

As they danced in silence, everything around them disappeared. The case disappeared. Judah's fears disappeared.

Piper leaned her head toward Judah, whispered in his ear. "You can't make decisions for someone else, Judah. That isn't love. I learned that the hard way in the last relationship I was in. I thought he loved me but love shouldn't look or feel like control."

Judah pulled her closer. She laid her head down into the crook of his shoulder, her breath on his neck. He never wanted to let her go.

He was going to kiss her again. He knew it seconds before he gave in to the desire, leaned his face down to hers. Judah had thought nothing could ever top those first few, but he had been wrong. Those had been a surprise to both of them. This one was intentional, slow and thought-out.

Perfect.

Piper pulled away and they both slowed to a stop, movements in sync when the song ended. And then they were standing there on the floor, Judah looking down at her, her face asking him so many questions he couldn't answer.

What were they doing? He didn't know.

Did he love her?

Judah was afraid he knew the answer to that. Afraid it was yes.

Sure, it was yes, if he was honest with himself. He was *in* love with her, too, but even more encompassing, he loved her. Full stop. No expectations, nothing.

Maybe, like that song earlier said, he had never stopped and had been pretending. But not just with her, with himself, too.

He loved her. And he would tell her…soon. He didn't want the case hanging over their heads, didn't want her wondering if it was something he'd said in the romantic moment. He wanted her to know he meant it.

And maybe he was still a little scared.

"Our food is probably ready," Piper finally murmured.

He made himself let her go and she moved away from him, her eyes not meeting his anymore. They walked back to the table and he noticed she was blushing.

As they settled back down, Judah found himself wishing they were still out there on the floor. He'd never been much of a dancer and would have said before to-night that it wasn't his thing. But being out there with Piper in his arms, nothing but them and the music, everything else disappearing in a background haze, made him feel like he could dance again and again. As long as he was with her.

"You okay?" Piper asked.

Judah realized the expression on his face was…well, probably weird. "Yeah." He smiled. "Fine. Why?" If he was Levi, he'd just tell her how he felt. That was what Levi had done with Adriana. He probably hadn't wrestled with this kind of hesitation, but Judah wasn't like his brother.

Maybe in this realm, that wasn't a good thing. Maybe in his personal life, taking a risk would be a good thing after all.

The drive home was quiet, much like the drive to the diner had been. But this felt different to Piper. Earlier it hadn't been a companionable silence, but she would have said it was fairly comfortable anyway. This silence felt heavy, like something was on Judah's mind that he didn't want to talk to her about. After all he'd said in the diner, after learning how he almost expected love not to last, and for people to disappoint him, she was even more curious what the silence meant.

Did he trust her with his heart? He knew she'd never do anything to intentionally cause him pain, didn't he?

"Everything all right?" she finally asked him.

"Yeah. I'm fine," he said in a voice that did not sound to Piper like he was fine at all.

They pulled into Levi and Adriana's driveway and Judah sighed. A deep, heavy sigh.

"Seriously." She shifted her weight so that she faced him. "What is it? I know today didn't lead to any kind of big breakthrough, but we made progress."

"It isn't that."

"What?"

He was quiet for a minute, then opened his door. "Let's talk about it inside. I don't like you being out here where you're an easy target."

Tired as Piper was, she noticed Judah sounded exhausted, too, and not just the kind that a good night's sleep could fix. Did she want to know what was wrong? What if it was her? Everything had seemed so perfect in the diner. For a second she'd thought…well, something that looked very much like love had shone in his eyes as they danced and she'd thought he might say so. He hadn't.

Now what had felt like romantic tension building between them felt almost like they'd gone backward. This felt like…fear?

Was Judah afraid of being in a relationship with her? Afraid for her because of this case?

They walked inside the house and the first thing Piper noticed was a note from Adriana that she and Levi had gone out for dinner and would be home around ten. It was only nine.

Maybe she was overly suspicious, but she couldn't help but wonder if her friend had wanted to give them time alone. She knew that Judah would never leave until someone else was there with her, preferably someone with law enforcement training and a gun.

Piper walked to the kitchen to make them both hot chocolate. It was becoming something of a nightly ritual. When she was home, Piper ran at night. Here she drank hot chocolate. The contrast wasn't lost on her. Still, it was worth it. Even more, the company was worth it. She'd enjoyed this time with Judah.

Funny how something she'd have been sure was only bad—her life in peril—could have led to having this new kind of friendship with Judah that was unlike any relationship she'd ever had before.

Did You do that, God? she wondered. Piper loved God, but sometimes forgot how much He was at work in her life. This had His fingerprints on it, though.

The idea that the God in charge of the universe cared enough about her life to be involved in it was hard to even wrap her mind around. She didn't deserve that kind of attention from Him, did she?

Or maybe it didn't matter. Maybe He gave it anyway?

It had been months after the relationship with Drew imploded before Piper realized how much a bad relationship with a person could impact someone's view of God. She still wasn't sure of what she believed was true or not true. It was something she needed to think through some more, but it didn't seem like quiet moments were very abundant in her life lately.

Piper finished making the hot chocolate and carried both mugs back into the living room, where Judah was sitting. She handed him one and sat down. Judah, who'd been sort of pacing the room, sat down right beside her.

What she really wanted was to ask him again what was wrong, but Judah wasn't the kind of man who responded well to being pushed and prodded. It would be best for her to wait until he told her.

They sat in silence for a while while Piper thought about the day. Some of it had been quieter than usual, and some of it full of more highs and lows than one day should have, and honestly, she was still reeling from it. He probably was, too.

Especially that dance…

It made sense to Piper, the reasons Judah had told her he had decided against being in a relationship. Piper appreciated that he cared enough about marriage to hold it in such high regard. But she also thought he was putting unnecessary restrictions on himself. It seemed like he was starting to agree with her; at least, that was what his kiss at the diner had said to her, but kisses could say a lot of things they didn't mean.

Had he meant it?

Did he still care about her?

Piper wanted to ask, to get it all out into the open, but she knew that wasn't the right choice here. She felt almost an extraordinary calm instead, as she sat on the couch and waited to see what Judah would say, to see what was on his mind.

To see if the answer had anything to do with her.

FIFTEEN

"Thanks for earlier," Piper finally said, before she took another sip of hot chocolate. "I had a lot of fun. I had no idea you could dance like that."

"Me, neither." Judah smiled. "I don't think I usually can. I think it was all you."

"We dance well together." Judah heard all kinds of things in that statement. He loved that Piper didn't mince words. She didn't try to pretend she wasn't feeling things that she was. Piper, in other words, was brave in all the places where he tended to give in to fear.

And tonight Judah wanted to be brave, too.

"I still don't know how this could look," he finally said after a deep breath.

"What?" She blinked up at him. He thought he saw the hint of a smile in her eyes, though, like she knew what he was getting at but was just waiting for him to say it.

And he should. It was part of being brave, and after all, didn't Piper deserve to actually hear a man say how he felt about her?

"I want another chance, Piper. I'm not saying I deserve it. I handled last time badly. You and I had just started getting to know each other when Levi started having huge problems in his marriage. I watched him get divorced and never wanted that to happen, so I did the easy thing. I just ran."

"You're not a runner, Judah. You're braver than that."

"I appreciate it." He paused. "But that time I wasn't. And I've regretted it ever since."

"You never gave any indication of it. All those times we worked together, you acted like you barely remembered me. Once or twice I wasn't even sure you did."

Judah winced. He was better at playing his feelings close to the vest than he thought, apparently, and he felt bad that he had done such a good job that Piper had gone through that. He couldn't imagine how he would have felt if the tables had been turned and he had ever wondered if she even knew who he was.

"The truth is, I never could have forgotten you." Now that he'd finally gotten up the courage to say something, anything, the words seemed like they wouldn't stop coming. "No one..." Judah swallowed hard. "No one has ever meant as much to me as you, Piper. And if you, if you want to try again...if you'll let me try again..." He blew out a breath. "I would really like to date you. I want to get to know you over coffee and ask you questions and hear about your past and tell you about me. I want to take you for walks in the rain and hikes and sit with you beside a fire late at night and talk about the future." His heart was pounding in his chest now as he watched her for her reaction.

Her smile was light, as it always was, and this one stretched slowly across her entire face. Still half-afraid she would reject him, Judah watched as she set her hot chocolate down on the table beside the couch, and then moved closer to him. Closer.

Closer.

The other kisses, he had started. He had finished.

This one was all Piper. Her lips were soft and smooth, exploring his like she had all the time in the world, like they were in no hurry at all.

She pulled away. Smiled again.

"I would love to get to know you better, Judah. If you want to date…I'm all in."

He finally took a full, deep breath.

Thank You, he said to God. God had given him courage, given him a second chance with Piper. He couldn't thank Him enough for those things.

Piper and Judah sat on the couch for another half hour or so, her cuddled into his shoulder, just drinking their hot chocolate and not saying anything at all. Judah couldn't believe she was willing to try again, but he wasn't about to talk her out of it. He was too thankful.

Still, he hadn't told her what had been on his mind on the drive home. It had been his initial idea for her to help with the case. And it was true that Judah had needed her help and their investigation had benefited from it. But the closer they got to the truth, the more dangerous it seemed, and the stronger Judah felt for Piper. At this point, asking her to continue with the investigation seemed foolish. She'd avoided being hurt or worse so far, but Judah didn't want to keep risking her life. It was too important for that.

He didn't know what she'd say about that, though. Judah hoped she understood. As difficult as it had been to have that conversation, to feel like he was risking his heart, using Piper was something that would bring more pain than he could imagine.

The decision had already been made. It was the only one he could make in good conscience, and the only one his heart could handle.

"Tomorrow I'm going to have a couple of officers from RPPD come here and stay with you," he finally said.

Piper frowned. It wasn't what she'd been expecting. "Okay…" Her mind was still processing.

"I don't want you to work the case anymore," he finished.

Piper frowned, let the words settle in. "At all?"

"At all. I didn't like how close it was the other day when we went in the river. This is the only way to make sure that doesn't happen again."

"I disagree. I'm just as much in danger anywhere at this point." Piper didn't like it, but it did seem like it was true. "I want to keep working it."

"You don't get a vote here."

"In my own life?" Piper stood up, needing the space between them. Her face had tensed into a frown as soon as the last sentence he'd spoken had come out. Had they gone so quickly from optimistic and in love to this? Judah wasn't the controlling sort; she'd been so sure of it. "Are you kidding me, Judah? That's not how this works!"

"How what works?"

"Having a relationship with someone." She spewed

the words out, watched their impact as Judah's face changed and fell.

"You're right." He was looking right at her, meeting her eyes, but there was no trace of the connection they'd had just half an hour earlier. Instead his expression was somber. "It's not how that works. But my first priority is to keep you safe, Piper. Maybe I wasn't wise to try to have a relationship with you while I was still working the case, but…"

"You can't do that."

"Keep you safe? Yes, I can."

"You can't, Judah. And you can keep trying, and I hope you succeed, but ultimately God is the one who decides how this all ends. He's protecting me." The words surprised her when they came out of her mouth, but she realized they were true. This experience was allowing her faith to grow back, replacing some of what had been damaged while she was dating Drew.

He shrugged.

Shrugged.

It was too familiar for Piper, having her opinions shrugged off, being told what to do, having decisions made for her about her *own life*. Judah was right. They shouldn't be doing this. Couldn't be doing this.

"You were right before. You *don't* know how to have a relationship." Piper took aim and released the words.

Judah said nothing.

It appeared that they had the impact she'd intended, but instead of making her feel less pain, she only felt more. Now she was hurting and so was he.

Piper ran to her borrowed room and shut the door.

Now all she could do was cry and hope he solved this

case. Because she never wanted to work closely with Judah Wicks again. Not after coming so close to happily-ever-after with him. She'd never met another man like him, certainly never kissed another man like him.

And they'd both detonated a bomb before their romance had much of a chance to begin. They'd both made their choices, said things they should have thought through more. She had been so sure that Judah was different, that he wasn't the kind of guy to make decisions about her life for her or act like she shouldn't have her own thoughts. But wasn't what he was doing the same thing Drew had done to her?

Even if he was doing it for her own good, Piper didn't think she could handle that. He would always think he knew best, and that was too similar to what she'd been through before.

Wasn't it? Even now, Piper's emotions warred against each other. Was it hopeless between them? She didn't know.

But it felt like it right now.

Somehow, Piper was going to have to figure out how to be content with her life the way it had been a mere week ago. Before Judah had walked back into her life and showed her what it could be like.

Before she'd started thinking about forever.

Love.

What did either of them know about love?

It didn't feel like Piper should have any more tears left, but they kept falling, dancing down her cheeks in rivers, hours later. She was home now, in the security of her own room. Whether it had been a wise decision to leave the safety of Levi and Adriana's house was debatable, but Piper hadn't wanted to be there anymore, in a place with such a connection to Judah. She'd wanted to be home, so that's where she'd gone, and where she was now, her thoughts still spinning in circles, her emotions still in turmoil.

Judah's motivations and Drew's were different; that was the thought she kept coming back to. Was she right? Probably? She didn't know anymore. The last thing she wanted was to be one of those women who fell into a cycle and couldn't get out, who lied to themselves about what they were experiencing, who excused a man's behavior to their own harm.

But Judah wasn't…wouldn't…

He'd made choices for her, without her permission. He'd left her out of a case that he'd invited her into. And he'd justified himself by saying he knew what was best.

Piper couldn't live like that again. She had come too far to go back to that woman she'd been years ago. In fact, she wouldn't recognize herself if she became that again.

She swiped at her cheeks, angry at all of it. She was angry that she'd gotten her hopes up, that she had really thought…

Well, she had thought she loved him. And that he loved her.

And that maybe she was going to get a happily-ever-after. How ridiculous was that?

Drew's voice echoed in her ears. *You don't deserve to be happy. You don't deserve to be treated any better.* Those and other familiar, cruel statements ran through her mind, and Piper did her best to block them out. But how did you unlearn lies you had been told and then clung to as truth?

She pulled the covers over her head, knowing that even though it was only just past five in the morning, it wasn't likely that she would get any more sleep.

Eventually she'd give up on sleep and go downstairs, but she wasn't very eager to now. Judah had sent over multiple cops since she'd insisted on going back to her own house. Adriana hadn't been thrilled with her for leaving, but even though they were friends it still felt weird to stay with Judah's brother when she and Judah were hardly even speaking anymore.

There was an officer outside her house, patrolling the perimeter, and one inside downstairs. Hence her lack of eagerness to leave her room. It would be strange enough on a normal day to have someone aware of all your activities, but on a day like today, when she just wanted to be alone and cry over what might have been and wasn't, Piper couldn't imagine facing other people just yet.

She'd just started to nod off again when her phone buzzed on the bedside table. She ignored it the first time, but when it went silent and then started going off again, she grew concerned, reached for it and answered.

"Hello?"

"Piper, it's Jake. I know I promised we wouldn't call unless we absolutely needed you."

Piper was already throwing back the covers and grabbing a pair of hiking pants to pull on. "But?"

"We need you."

"Fourteen-Mile River?"

She heard the hesitation in Jake's voice. "No. Someone tried to walk out on the mudflats."

Even worse. Everyone from Raven Pass, down at the farthest corner of Turnagain Arm up to Anchorage at its mouth, knew about the danger of the mudflats. Still, every summer people insisted on walking in them. The thick glacial silt acted like fast-setting concrete when it got wet and there were decades of horror stories of the horrible ways people had died when they'd become trapped.

It was a slow, painful way to go, one where the person dying was fully conscious as the tide rose and took away their hope one wave at a time.

And then they were gone.

"I'm on my way."

"Piper." Jake blew out a breath. "I hated to even call you. I don't know, could it be a trap? Judah told me the basic gist of why someone is after you a couple days ago, and I told myself I wouldn't call you in for any reason, because I don't want to risk putting you in danger. But it's at the mouth of Fourteen-Mile River. You and I are the only ones who can operate the boat and I'd rather have both of us there in case anything goes wrong. But it's a risk. I don't know who is stuck out there and I don't know how they got there."

She was pulling her shoes on now. "But someone is for sure out there?"

"That's what the caller reported."

Unease ate at Piper's gut. It could be a trap. But she couldn't let fear for her own life keep her from doing her job. And she didn't have time to deliberate.

"And how long until high tide?"

"A few hours," Jake said.

It sounded like a lot of time, but Piper knew it wasn't.

This was a do-or-die kind of situation, one where Piper didn't have any extra time to make decisions. Those decisions were heavy with the weight of someone else's life.

"I'm on my way."

"Piper?"

"Yeah?"

"Be careful."

Piper hung up the phone and hurried down the stairs, then briefly explained to the officer assigned to her where she was going. As she'd expected, the woman wasn't thrilled. And Piper understood. The last thing she wanted to do was to be foolish and take risks that weren't necessary when the stakes were so high. But this was her job, something that meant a lot to her, and more important, it was someone's life on the line.

What about your life? She could almost hear Judah's voice in her head. But last night, Judah had lost all right to have a say in her decisions.

Checking outside carefully, Piper walked to her car and started it up. As she'd expected, one of the officers climbed into the squad car and prepared to follow her. That was fine with her. They wouldn't be able to be with her all the way to the river, but she'd take any kind of backup she could have.

Jake sometimes carried a gun with him, more for bears than anything else, but that could help also.

She was lying to herself, Piper knew. She was sugarcoating the danger in an attempt to justify what she was doing. It was funny, she thought as she drove, how she could separate herself from the situation and see what she was doing, make value judgments about it. It was probably an indicator that she was doing something she shouldn't be doing, or that at the least she was doing something that was worth more thought, but this had a time limit attached to it. The tide was already on its way in. She had no more time.

Piper parked at SAR headquarters to find Jake hitching up the trailer. She helped him finish up and then climbed into the back seat of the truck. Ellie was already in the front seat. Ellie was a strong team member.

"All right." Jake climbed in and started driving. Piper looked back to see that the Raven Pass Police Department squad car was behind them. "We got the call half an hour ago. High tide is now two and a half hours away."

"How far into the arm are they?"

Jake shook his head. "I'm not sure."

"You took the call?" Piper asked.

He nodded. "Remember? I told you someone called it in."

Dread started to build inside her. "It wasn't the person who was stuck who called?"

Memories of Randy, the intoxicated man in the canoe, made dread creep over Piper's shoulders. It had been called in fast, fast enough that Piper had actually been able to save him. Someone had called this rescue in at three hours to high tide. Just enough time to think they had the chance to perform a rescue. It involved water, something Piper was good at. Her specialty.

Everything pointed to it being like the others. Someone else being killed, but this time Piper was being lured there intentionally to kill her, too.

Maybe. Was she overreacting? Letting fear control her? How much fear was healthy and how much wasn't?

Her thoughts turned to the potential victim. Who

was this victim, she wondered, and what connection did he or she have to the mine?

"I can't do this," she heard herself say, her rapidly pounding heart rate making her chest feel constricted. "I'm sorry, Jake. I think you were right to say it might be a trap."

"You think?" He looked over at her.

"Piper, if you're wrong…" Ellie didn't have to finish the sentence. Piper got it. If she was wrong, her not being there would complicate the rescue and could cost someone their life.

But at some point, didn't she need to acknowledge that her life was worth saving, too? That no matter how much she tried to prove her worth by saving other people…

She was already worth something. To God.

Her value wasn't tied to Drew. Wasn't tied to Judah.

God said she mattered.

God, don't You want me to try to save someone, though? I want to do this for You. I want—

Piper didn't see the oncoming car until right when it swerved into their lane, clipping them from the side. She heard her screams, Ellie's, Jake's, as the SUV tumbled off the road, the trailer throwing them even more off balance. The river wasn't far in that direction, and if they went over the cliff, they'd land in the river—for sure.

The car landed hard and stopped. Piper's mind swam. Her head throbbed. She could taste blood in her mouth.

Had someone hit them on purpose or had they truly been in an accident? Piper didn't know what to think anymore.

Except that she wished Judah was here, she thought as she lost consciousness.

SIXTEEN

Judah had been needed on patrol, so he was having to take a forced break from Piper's case. Maybe it wasn't such a bad thing, because his mind was already heavy with her and with regret. Thinking about her even more wasn't going to help.

Not that he had been able to avoid thinking about her on patrol, either. He drove past the crag where they'd first climbed together and wished they could do it again. Then he drove through a few little Raven Pass neighborhoods and noticed a couple walking with a toddler.

His mind had done all kinds of things with that one. What would it have been like to marry Piper? To actually make it work and have a family together?

Judah wasn't a quitter and he hadn't wanted to give up on Piper, but when she'd told him to leave last night she'd seemed pretty certain, so he'd left. It wasn't until he'd gotten home that he wondered if he should have fought harder, should have made sure she knew that walking away from her was the last thing he wanted. But he'd hurt her when he'd told her he was going to work the case alone.

Wasn't that what love did? Didn't it protect people? Or was he protecting Piper from possible hurt when that really wasn't his job?

God, I don't understand how this is supposed to work, but I know that I love her. Please don't let me lose her.

He had really thought this was his second chance. And he had wanted it to work so badly.

The scanner crackled. An accident had just happened on Birch Street, above Fourteen-Mile River, and police presence was required.

Judah turned around and headed in that direction, doing his best to keep his mind on his job. "Unit Eight responding," he said into the radio.

More chatter on the scanner. The vehicle was being described. Judah turned up the volume and listened.

It was the Raven Pass SAR team SUV, with the boat and trailer.

Piper wasn't working, though. She should still be at home with the officers he'd sent over there.

So why did it feel like his heart had dropped into his stomach? Surely he was overreacting. Except it didn't feel that way. He pressed down harder on the gas, wishing it was possible to get to the scene of the accident even faster. Thankfully, Raven Pass was a small town, so it wouldn't be more than about three more minutes, but when minutes mattered, three felt like too many.

She had to be okay.

Judah pulled up to the scene. Other officers were on the scene, and they were already working on pulling people out of the vehicle.

First was Ellie Connors. Judah hurried over to help

and was there when they got Jake Stone out of the driver's side. His temple was bleeding and while he was conscious, he looked to be in the worst shape. It made sense, given the fact that the driver's side had borne the brunt of the impact.

"That's all," an officer said; Judah didn't see who. "Vehicle is clear."

"No." Jake moaned the word as an EMT who had just arrived loaded him onto a stretcher. "Piper was here."

Piper was...

"Judah!" He heard the scream but didn't see her. The area was becoming more crowded with people, as traffic had slowed down at the accident site. The movement was dizzying as Judah turned his head left, then right, searched the trees and brush for some sign of Piper.

His gaze went to the river. No sign of anyone in there, which was good. Piper had managed to get out safely the other day, but to defy the odds twice would be remarkable. Besides that, there was a possibility she was injured from the car wreck.

Judah didn't want to think about how badly she could be hurt and definitely didn't want to think about how she could have disappeared from the crash site.

Except it was obvious. She hadn't walked away on her own. So someone had taken her. Most likely the person they had been searching for this whole time.

God, please let her be okay. Judah felt his shoulders tense and took a deep breath. Adrenaline did funny things to people. He couldn't afford for it to mess him up right now.

He pulled his phone out of his pocket and dialed the

police chief. "I'm at Fourteen-Mile River. Piper is missing and I think she's been abducted."

The chief asked him a few questions; Judah clarified things and slid the phone in his pocket. Then he thought better of it and texted Levi. Piper is missing. At Birch Street accident. Help. He'd so rarely asked his brother for aid, his *little* brother, that it still felt strange. But this wasn't the time to let his pride make decisions for him. Judah wanted as good a chance as possible to find Piper safe.

He hurried into the brush near the river, walked closer toward the water. On this side, the land rose into a bluff. He could walk down to the river if he went south a little, but from where he was, there was a drop. He didn't want to get too close to the edge.

How could he have let this happen? He'd wanted to keep Piper safe, had wanted it so desperately he'd sacrificed maybe the only chance he'd had of a happily-ever-after with her.

He'd been wrong to make decisions for her, wrong to refuse to discuss his fears with her. He loved her. He trusted her with his life. Surely he should have had enough faith to trust her with her own.

He should have loved her better. Then maybe she wouldn't have left. Maybe she wouldn't be in danger right now.

Judah's stomach felt ill. He had to find her. Had to.

"Judah!" he heard again.

From below. Judah blinked and then took off running to where he could access the river's shoreline. He made the hundred-yard-or-so run as quickly as he could, his mind working all the way. If he remembered correctly, a thin strip of beach ran along most of this side, under the rocks. Was it possible Piper was down there?

When he was beside the river he looked up, his gaze going up the cliffside. The car wreck was somewhere near the highest point of that. It was good they hadn't rolled any farther. That was something he didn't even want to think about.

A recovery mission for Piper would have been more than he could handle. His chest hurt just thinking about it, so he shoved the thought out of his mind and did his best to focus on what was actually happening.

There. What was that on the cliffside? There was a small ledge, twenty feet or so from the top of the cliff, maybe two feet in depth, and that looked like the crumpled form of a person.

Oh, please. His heart clenched. She had to be alive. *Had to be.*

Please, God.

Judah sprinted in that direction until he ran out of sandy beach, then looked up. She was to his right and above him, probably fifteen feet farther than he was able to walk on the riverbank, and thirty-five feet up, on that ledge. He'd heard her voice calling to him five minutes ago, so he didn't know what to think about the fact that she'd stopped calling for him. Had she fallen and lost consciousness after she called his name?

Or...

No. He couldn't think that way. Could. Not.

But he had to get to her and he didn't have time to waste. He didn't have his harness, and even if he did, he hadn't brought what he needed to safely belay himself.

The rock was good for Alaska, big holds. But there

was always the danger of some coming loose. Judah hadn't climbed here before, mostly because he preferred sport climbing and this wall wasn't bolted yet.

But it looked easy enough. He thought he could see a climbable line, one that was well within his range of abilities. Still, all of that was figuring on him having a harness on. And before he could even climb that, he'd have to traverse over, climbing sideways over the river. If he fell from there, the options ranged from becoming paralyzed if he hit a rock on the bottom of the river wrong, to drowning.

Either way, death seemed likely.

So, while the climbing looked well within his skills, maybe 5.8, he'd rate it an R for danger. Climbers tended to tack on ratings like movies. PG-13 meant you'd get seriously hurt. R usually meant death was likely if you fell.

In a case like that, there was only one option.

Don't fall.

Judah lifted his hands to the rock and hoped he wasn't overestimating his skills. He wouldn't be helping Piper if he got himself killed. She was counting on him. And more than anything, Judah didn't want to let her down.

His forearms were pumped, the blood flowing to them so much they were almost past the point of use. If Judah were climbing for fun right now, he would call it quits. But this wasn't just any climb and it wasn't for fun. Piper was depending on him. He still didn't know for sure what kind of shape she was in, and he knew that in a situation like she was in, time mattered. She could have injuries that needed attention. There was no way of knowing until he was up there.

Had backup arrived? He hadn't seen any signs of her would-be killers when he'd started the climb, but right now he wasn't able to look around much. Honestly, he couldn't even think much about the case or Piper. Helping her right now meant sending this climb, and that could only be done by focusing on his movements, his breathing, and the rock.

He reached up with his left hand, pressed his thumb into the rough surface enough to hold himself on and lifted his right leg high. He adjusted his toes, shifted his weight slightly on his foot and took a deep breath. He'd made it through that move, but his arms were starting to quiver. Judah looked up. Ten feet left. Maybe eight. It was difficult to judge distances and they really didn't matter. Right now all he needed was to get there, get his hands up on the ledge and mantle up to where Piper was. And pray she didn't move when he was climbing up and knock him down.

Had he passed the crux of the route? Also not something he needed to think about, he reminded himself, focusing on the gray-brown rock, the rough texture. Not as smooth as granite, but smoother than some of the unstable, jagged rock farther north in the state. Shiny bits of something, maybe mica in it, he thought as he moved. Left arm to that jug, switch his feet, move right, reach with the right hand. There, that hold.

Two feet. He made the moves with confidence, knowing that hesitation on a hold could mean failure. For him, moving was the best way to ensure he climbed a route. If he hesitated too long, he often made mistakes. Finally, *finally*, Judah reached up to the ledge and mantled up to it. Piper was lying there, eyes closed. She had several scrapes on her arms. No wounds on her head that he could see, but those weren't always visible.

She was lying there, so still.

For a second, he was afraid he would stop breathing.

But no, he kept on inhaling, his lungs burning from the exertion of the climb, arms aching, heart pounding in his chest. He was exhausted but he was fully, gloriously alive, and he wanted Piper to be, too.

She had to be.

Judah knelt beside her. "Piper." He laid a hand on her arm, moved her gently. No response. Realizing he had no choice, he reached for her wrist to feel for a pulse, his chest tightening with every second that went by. He waited, adjusted his grip because he'd never been that good at finding a pulse on someone else.

There was her heartbeat, strong in her wrist.

Judah felt his shoulders relax immediately.

Except that they were still up on a ledge with no easy way down. He'd kept that in the back of his mind during the climb up and had tried to assess whether or not they could get down the same way. Judah thought they could, but it wasn't a foolproof plan. It certainly had its hazards.

And it wasn't what he needed to be thinking through right now. At the moment, he needed to figure out how to wake Piper up. Whoever had pushed her to the ledge, presumably the killer, could be coming back at any moment. They weren't safe here.

"Piper," he said again, his voice urgent.

Please, God, wake her up. We have to get down.

For a second he wondered if it was coincidence, before he realized that no, God deserved the credit. Because no sooner had he finished praying than Piper's eyelids fluttered open.

"You found me," she said and his heart broke and healed all in those three words. Because yes, he had. He'd found her—the *one* he hadn't been looking for in life but that God knew he'd needed.

And because of God he'd found her right now also, literally.

"What happened? Are you hurt?" It was a dumb question because she clearly had a head injury. The passing out seemed to indicate that pretty clearly. But he needed to know and he needed something to keep her talking, keep her awake.

"I'm okay," she said, blinking like she didn't quite believe her own words. "I'm okay. I think. My head hurts." She sat up, reached her arms out, moved around a little. "Nothing else hurts any more than it should."

"What happened?"

Piper shook her head. "We got into a wreck. Judging by how fast the man pulled me out of the car and hauled me away, I have to believe it was intentional."

"Did you get a look at who it was?" If so, she might have the knowledge to end this right now, and he could arrest whoever had been responsible for the killings and attempted murder. Judah would sleep so much better when the man or woman was in jail.

"I didn't." She shook her head. "He had on a mask."

"He?"

"The person was a man, I'm sure from the build. Anyway, he was pulling me this way and then I started fighting. I guess we got too close to the edge. While we were fighting, I got in one good hit, unprotected. It was enough to make him cry out, but it also meant that I got close enough that he grabbed my wrist and threw me this direction. I went over the side of the cliff and fell here." She frowned. "I might have blacked out at first, but I woke up and called for you."

"I heard you. That's how I found you," he said.

She smiled a little. "I knew you would."

There was so much he wanted to say, so many things he had avoided talking about that he wanted to address now. He could see that he'd done the same thing with their relationship that he'd done with the case. Judah was so afraid of Piper getting hurt that he wanted to protect her, but making decisions for her didn't make her feel protected.

He'd messed up. He'd really messed up. And he probably would again, many times. But he wanted to talk to Piper and see if she wanted to give "them" a chance.

However, there was nothing romantic or practical about having that conversation on the side of a cliff. And they had to hurry to shelter, because he wasn't giving the killer another chance at Piper.

"But you're really okay?" he confirmed again.

"Yes, why?"

"Well…" Judah trailed off.

"Oh. We have to get down somehow."

"The SAR team could probably rappel down to us, if they hadn't just been in a wreck. And they may be okay…"

"But as it stands you want to try to find another way," she said, understanding. "Okay." She leaned over the edge slightly. Judah understood what she was doing, just trying to see, but it was too much leaning for him. He pushed her back.

Rather than looking annoyed, she smiled at him. "Sorry, I was just thinking. So we're forty feet up?"

"Maybe a little less. I guessed thirty-five. You fell about twenty feet earlier, and it was enough to knock you unconscious."

"So if we can downclimb even half of it successfully, we won't die. Oh, well, I guess we would fall in the river." Piper frowned and looked back at Judah. "Did you have to traverse to get up here?"

"Yeah, I came from that little strip of beach down there." He pointed.

"Then we'll go back down there."

"You sure you can do it?" He was concerned about staying up here, completely exposed on the rock, but he was concerned about pushing them to do something dangerous also.

How could both options feel so dangerous and foolish? Didn't there have to be a right answer? Apparently not; at least, that was the way life felt.

"I can." She grinned, just a little, but enough to reassure Judah she was really okay. "The question is, can you?"

"Okay, easy there, tiger. Let's not give me a complex." He laughed. If she was joking, that had to be a good sign, didn't it?

"Sorry."

But she didn't look like it and Judah was thankful. He needed her in this kind of mood, lighthearted and apparently ready to conquer the world. Later there would be time to be serious, look at how to identify the man who had abducted her and pushed her over the edge. There might even be time for him to tell her how he really felt about her.

I love you, Piper, he thought to himself, wishing he could say the words, hear them come out of his mouth.

Not yet. It wasn't time.

Judah was so tired of being afraid.

"All right, for the down climb, here's the line I think will work best." Judah motioned to the rock below them and pointed out some of the features to Piper that she could use to make her way down.

"It's got good holds," she said. "Nice and big, just a little chunky. Did anything pull out of the rock when you climbed up? Is it chossy and breakable at all?"

"I didn't have any problems."

She nodded. "Okay, let's do this. Who first?"

"Me," Judah said, not because he wanted to leave her alone on the ledge for another second, but because he wanted to be below her. If anyone was going to catch anyone else's fall, it was going to be him catching hers.

Because love wasn't about making decisions for someone or taking away their voice. It was protecting them where you could, sacrificing for them, living out your love in little everyday acts.

Maybe...maybe now was the time.

"Piper?" Judah started before he could lose his nerve.

"Yeah?" Her eyes searched his.

"We'll talk later, but...I love you."

Judah moved backward, felt with his heel for the holds as he lowered himself down by his arms. His biceps protested, but he ignored them, and within seconds, he was positioned well on the wall. Okay, so far so good. If he could just go back down the way he'd come up...

"You coming?" he asked Piper when he was about ten feet down, with plenty of room above him for her to lower herself.

"On my way. And, Judah? I love you, too," she said in a voice so confident Judah could have kissed her right then. How could one woman be so many things? Confident and uncertain, bold and brave and still willing to be taken care of?

God had done a fantastic job of creating Piper McAdams. Judah would be thankful for her every single day of his life if he had his choice.

He *loved* her. He still couldn't get over that.

But before he could start thinking about what it would be like to love her for the rest of his life, he needed to get her down from this ledge, make sure they took care of the threat against her. *Then* they could move on. Discuss having a future.

Please help us get down safely and catch him fast, Judah prayed, meaning every word.

SEVENTEEN

Piper felt breathless but didn't know if it was from Judah or the climb. Oh, Judah. She couldn't think about him right now—she had to stay focused—but she had no idea how she was supposed to when he'd said that to her right before their down climb. He *loved* her? Truly?

That was bigger than a couple of incredible kisses, better than putting himself in danger every day to keep her safe. That was words that backed up so many actions she'd seen him take in relation to her. And Piper had no idea how much it would mean for her to hear them.

Focus, Piper. Her arm muscles were screaming at her. They'd been tired enough from their climbing yesterday and now they were being asked to do one of the hardest climbing skills—downclimbing—when she was already past the post of exhaustion. Her head throbbed from her fall. She needed a hot shower and a nap.

Still, she put one foot ahead of the other, slowly feeling her way down the wall. Judah was right below her, and Piper knew it was because he had decided he would rather break her fall than let her break his. Well, he should know she wasn't going to fall. Not now.

"Now you're going to move left along the wall. You should like this part—it has little crimpy holds."

Judah was right, that was her preferred style, but Piper hadn't done much downclimbing. She usually just rappelled. She certainly didn't downclimb free soloing.

"Hey, wait."

Judah stopped.

"Oh, sorry, I didn't mean literally. I just realized something."

"What's that?"

"You free soloed for me. You literally did the riskiest thing in climbing, just to save me." The man who was so careful, who valued safety so much, had completely ignored his own in order to ensure hers.

Yes, his motivations for taking her off the case, for being overbearing, were honorable. She still wished he hadn't done it and wished he'd talked to her about it, but...

She could believe him when he said he loved her. Judah meant it. He showed it in so many ways.

He smiled at her. Kept traversing.

Piper followed, ignoring her aching muscles. Finally, finally they were almost down. When she made it to sand, she let go and let herself collapse onto the ground. She needed a minute, two minutes, to catch her breath.

"You okay?" Judah asked.

Piper nodded. "I'm fine."

Movement caught her attention. It wasn't much, just a slight shift in something in her peripheral vision. Behind Judah.

"Not for long, though."

Piper recognized the voice. It was male. Maybe

midthirties. She'd heard it earlier today when her attacker had said something to her as he dragged her away from the search and rescue vehicle.

And now she realized she had heard it before that, when she and Judah had gone to talk to Randy Walcott.

She turned.

"Randy?"

The man standing behind them pulled his mask off, apparently deciding it wasn't doing any good anymore. It was Randy, standing there behind them. He must have been watching them climb and been waiting on the beach.

She looked over at Judah. She couldn't see a weapon on him, but it was possible he had concealed one.

Although, would he climb with a gun on him? Not likely. Piper felt helpless, which she hated, but she was aching, exhausted and not up for a fight for her life. She'd just worked things out with Judah. *Please*. It couldn't end like this.

God, please help us now. Please don't let us die today.

"Randy?" Judah frowned. "Who else at the mine are you helping?"

"What? You don't think I could do all this myself?" He gestured wildly with the gun he'd been hiding, his finger shoved through the trigger guard. "No one thinks I can handle anything myself, but here I am, handling things…"

His words slurred a little, and Piper wasn't sure he was completely sober. That could be to their advantage, if he'd had enough alcohol to dull his reflexes or response times. But it could be to their disadvantage.

"So wait…but you almost drowned?" Piper meant it as a statement but it came out as a question. Her head was still throbbing and her mind felt sluggish, like it had the pieces to put things together but just couldn't quite do it. She was sleepy, so sleepy, and realized she likely needed to get to the doctor to be seen for a head injury.

It was a strange thing to think when you were standing in front of a man with a large gun trained at you, but Piper felt like she was entitled to have some strange thoughts.

"I didn't. I set that up because I was going to drown you. It was going to be so easy. I'd been watching you. I knew if it was a water rescue, you'd break protocol and come immediately just to be able to save someone. I didn't mean to get quite as drunk as I did, just enough that I'd have alcohol in my system to explain my near drowning, but you did exactly what I thought. You came and saved me, threw suspicion off of me. Which was the least you could do, since you'd already ruined one of my planned eliminations."

"You mean murders?" Judah broke in.

Randy barely glanced in his direction. He seemed fixated on Piper. "You ruined it. You rescued that hiker, Jay Jones. You found the body of the woman I killed when she was camping. The whole SAR team kept getting in the way, but it was mostly you. I watched when you found the body, did you know that? And I saw how hard you worked and I thought…you could destroy my entire plan, so I knew you had to die. And I figured if I set myself up like a victim, well, even better, because it would draw suspicion off of me. But you rescued me at the lake. So I set up the rescue at the cliff, but you got away there, too. But I kept on coming after you, because you had to die."

"Had to…" Piper trailed off. She didn't want to finish that sentence. Not out loud, not in her head.

"Now you're going to die." He waved the gun around again for a few seconds, then slowly leveled the heavy barrel directly at Piper's chest.

"Wait." Judah's voice was strong. Deep. "You sound like you had a really thought-out plan. Can you tell me why you decided to do it?"

"You just want me to confess."

"You already have," Judah said. "I just think it seems like a guy who has put as much effort into this as you have deserves to tell his story."

Piper couldn't believe the way Randy straightened up, nodded once and seemed to be giving great consideration to what Judah had said. "Maybe I do." He considered. "Maybe I do."

"Why don't you tell us why you came up with all this? You work at the mine, so you just wanted to make operations easier by eliminating some of the sources of the discontent within the community?"

He shook his head. "No. I don't really get too much responsibility on my own there. I keep telling my Aunt Lisa I can handle it, to promote me, but does she? No. I thought if I helped her and got rid of some of the people who have been causing her problems, I could have a better job." Here he waved the gun again. "More power, more money."

The gun fired, the explosion echoing off the rock and down the river.

The bullet had hit a soft spot in the wall, splintering some layers of rock and making dirt fall in a steady stream down to the ground.

Then the world stilled again.

"So my aunt doesn't need me. But she does, she just doesn't want to admit it. There may be more people who need to have unfortunate accidents and I can't have Piper getting in the way anymore. Besides, you two… killing you will get people off my back about those murders and then I can just live my life. They both made their choices, those people who died. They chose to get in the way of progress, of the mine. So they had to die, too. It's not all my fault…" He trailed off.

Piper looked at Judah and wondered how much they could communicate nonverbally. If he was able to understand her expression well enough, maybe they could come up with some kind of plan. They definitely needed to disarm him. It would be best if they could restrain him somehow, also. Climbing rope would work well if they had any, but, well, if they'd had that they wouldn't have had to free solo.

"How about we go into town and talk about this? You sound like a guy who has been overlooked and I want to listen to you, give you a fair chance."

"A chance at what? You have to arrest me. And I'm not letting that happen."

Judah looked at him.

"We've talked enough." He moved to raise the weapon again slowly, but before he'd gotten it all the way to a ready stance height, a gun went off, the boom echoing.

Randy suddenly dropped to the ground. It was a clean shot, so Piper hoped medical professionals might be able to do something with it, help him somehow. She didn't want him to die, even though he'd tried to kill her.

Piper looked around for the source of the shot.

Levi stood on the beach, fifty feet away.

"Sorry I took so long to get here," he said as he walked in Judah's direction, closing the distance between them quickly.

"I'm glad you made it." Judah clapped his brother on the back. "Thanks for taking that shot."

"I didn't want to give things a chance to escalate any more. At least not with the case." Levi looked from Piper, to Judah.

The unspoken message was clear. He clearly thought something was escalating between Judah and Piper.

And actually, Piper thought he might be right.

Levi went to where Randy had fallen, began applying pressure to the wound.

Piper watched, her mind wrestling with the way police officers were trained to render aid, even if they'd had to be the ones to inflict harm to save someone else's life. It was a lot to wrap her mind around, but she knew it made sense. If she'd been called on right now to rescue Randy, she would have, even after all his attempts to kill her.

"You okay?" Judah asked her, wrapping his arm around her.

Piper nodded slowly. "Yeah. I'm okay. I hope he is."

"I'm glad we caught him and it's over."

"I am, too." Piper shook her head. "All of that because he felt overlooked by his aunt, who was the assistant manager?"

"And because the mine where he worked was threatened and he decided to take matters into his own hands and eliminate people who had spoken out against the mine's negative effects."

Piper let out a deep breath.

EMTs arrived on the scene then and took over for Levi.

"Let's get you guys debriefed so you can get out of here," Levi said, motioned toward where the cruisers were parked, back on the road.

Judah's heart was still pounding in his chest as he led Piper to where several Raven Pass PD cruisers had clustered. She'd be able to give her statement there and avoid going down to the department another time. She'd seen enough of the inside of police stations to last her the rest of her life, probably.

Chief Moore was waiting for them beside one of the cars. "Everybody okay?" he asked.

Piper looked at Judah and they both nodded. "Yes, sir. It was close, but we made it."

Closer than Judah would have liked, for sure. The image of Piper up there on the ledge would probably never be fully erased from his mind. But she was safe now.

And now he needed to face whatever was happening between them, for real, without the threat of danger, without adrenaline coursing through his veins. For him, this was going to take more courage than facing down a killer.

But it had the potential to have an incredible impact on his life.

"Can you tell me what happened, starting at the

crash?" The chief directed the words to Piper. Piper told him the details, and Judah grew more and more amazed that she was okay.

Could it be that God had been directing them? Not just keeping them safe, but being real and involved in their lives? Judah knew it was possible. It was what he had believed was true all his life. But sometimes when the unusual happened, it was hard to feel like it was true.

But today, he knew it was. Felt it deep inside his chest, to his core.

Thank You, God.

"Judah, how did you find her?" the chief was asking him. Judah briefed him, gave him all the details he had.

"Levi fired the shot that took the suspect down," Judah finished. All of them looked to the left, where Randy was being loaded into an ambulance. After he was attended to medically, he'd be going to prison, something that would help Judah sleep much better at night.

Chief Moore spoke. "We've got his gun in custody. I sent officers to his house and they found a rifle there the same caliber as the one that someone fired at the two of you at the police department. There's more work to do evidence-wise, but I think we've got enough to put him away. And since he knows he confessed to you anyway, it's likely he will just plead guilty."

Judah hoped so. He didn't want the man out of prison for as long as he lived, because he wanted Piper to be able to live in the full freedom of knowing that she was okay and there was no one out to get her.

Actually, there were a lot of things he wanted for Piper, but they hadn't had time to talk about any of them.

Chief Moore continued. "Thanks for everything you did today, Wicks. I think it might be time to start talking about a promotion."

With that, the chief walked away toward another group of officers, and Piper looked at Judah with her eyes wide.

"A promotion, huh? Do I get partial credit for helping you get that?" Her voice was teasing, her smile wide, though the crinkles around her eyes said she was tired. It had been an exhausting day.

"You think you should get credit?" Judah raised his eyebrows and grinned, then stepped toward her.

"I think if I hadn't been in danger you might not have worked so hard." Her words were honest and hit home. "I think you worked so hard because it was me."

Judah's face lost all hint of a smile as he stood there staring down at her. This was too important to joke about, and he wanted to make sure that with everything in her, she knew he wasn't teasing her.

"It was because of you that I worked so hard," he said in full honesty.

"I was kidding."

"But I wasn't." Judah reached out both hands for hers. She set them inside his and it felt so, so right. "I pride myself on doing a good job with my work, but this was personal to me. Doing everything I could to make sure that the threat against you went away was something I did because it was you, Piper."

"You said you loved me. On the rock." Her face asked

her questions for her, as it so often did, her blue eyes hopeful, but uncertain.

"I did say that. And I meant it." Judah blew out a breath. "Piper, I know I messed up by cutting you out of the case. I never wanted to boss you around or make decisions for you or make you feel controlled." He hesitated and tried to find the right words. "All I wanted was to keep you safe, but I guess I overstepped."

"I shouldn't have yelled at you. I handled it wrong, too."

"We're probably going to handle things wrong now and then. Maybe..." Judah trailed off. "Maybe sometimes people do and it's okay anyway."

"Judah?"

"Yeah?"

"You would never hurt someone on purpose. I know you better than that." Her voice was full of hope so strong that Judah could feel it.

And yeah, when she said it that way...he could almost believe she was right. Either way, he did believe that it was worth the risk. Maybe he wasn't the best at relationships, and it was hard to have a stressful job and maintain a good balance. But Piper was right. He would never hurt her on purpose. He couldn't make decisions for her.

And despite thinking he'd known exactly how his life was going to go, despite being sure he would just have to give up any dreams of having a wife one day, Judah thought he might have been wrong.

Because it turned out love really was worth the risk after all.

"I love you, Piper. Not just when everything is crazy

and we're in danger on the side of a cliff. I think I've loved you for longer than I've realized. And I want to love you for as long as I live."

She threw her arms around his neck so quickly that he almost didn't know what was happening, and when he'd regained his balance, Judah laughed.

The sound was one that would have surprised him just a week ago, but he was getting used to it now. It turned out that being around Piper made him laugh a lot. And he could get used to that. He hoped she was still making him laugh five, ten, twenty years from now.

For the rest of his life.

And that he could spend that time making her happy, too.

"I love you, too," she told him.

And Judah prayed, thanking God for letting him have this second chance, for showing him that there were some things worth fighting his fears for, and for Piper.

He thanked Him twice for Piper.

And then he pulled her in for a kiss. The first of many more to come.

Two weeks later, Piper was back at work. Jake had gotten a new car to replace the one that had been totaled in the wreck.

She'd seen Judah every night since then when he picked her up for dates, and some mornings, too, when he'd come by with coffee for her as a surprise at the end of his shifts. She'd laughed more these last couple of weeks than she ever had in her life.

There were still things to work out. Now and then

Piper found herself reverting to old habits, to apologizing too much for something, and Judah had to remind her that he wasn't like that. He wasn't Drew.

And he wasn't. In any way. He was Judah, and she was so very thankful for him.

"Day going okay?" Jake asked this morning as she walked in. Piper smiled at him. "It's going well so far." She smiled at Jake's wife, Cassie, who was a doctor in town but helped out often at the SAR headquarters. She and Jake seemed so happy, and if Piper wasn't mistaken, Cassie's stomach seemed a little rounder...

Cassie caught her looking at it. "Finally showing, huh?" She laughed. "I'm four months along."

"Oh my goodness. That's amazing, Cassie. Congrats, you guys! Jake, you didn't say anything!"

Her boss had walked into another room, but she heard him laughing. "Cassie told me she wanted to see how long it took for people to notice."

Piper thought they were funny. If she ever got married and became pregnant, she'd probably tell everyone within the first five minutes of knowing herself. She couldn't keep things like that from people, not good news.

"I'm going to go work on organizing the locker room." The SAR team members were on call for part of their workweek and in the station for the rest of the week, doing odd jobs around headquarters.

Piper walked past Ellie and waved to her, also. She was working at a desk.

And there was Adriana. Weird that her entire team was here today.

And Levi. Wait. Why was Levi here, too?

Piper had just turned around, trying to figure out what was going on, when Judah walked into the room, smiling. He was holding a bouquet of sunflowers.

She hadn't even known they were her favorite, until right now.

"Piper, I used to be kind of a loner."

Quiet laughter came from more than one place in the room. Possibly from everyone there.

"But when you came into my life, you brought sunshine, hence the flowers." He handed them to her. "You brought me into this group of friends," he said and nodded to the people around them. "And most of all, you brought me the best relationship I could ever hope to have. You gave me your life, Piper. Your smile. Your jokes. Your climbing tips. I could never explain how much you mean to me, but I want to spend the rest of my life trying, if you'll let me."

Piper felt her eyes widen as she caught her breath. Was he...

"Piper Alison McAdams," he started, "will you marry me?"

"I would love to," she said, a smile spreading across her face. He pulled her into his arms, almost crushing her against his firm chest, and Piper laughed.

"You're squishing me." He laughed but loosened his grip.

"Can't have that, now."

"You make me laugh, Judah Wicks."

"I hope to make you laugh for the rest of our lives," he said with a smile, another laugh escaping his lips.

And Piper knew that God had taken care of her and blessed her beyond what she could have ever dreamed.

Thank You, she prayed, and kissed the man who would be her husband soon.

Husband. She liked the sound of that.

"I love you."

"I love you, too. Forever."

Happily-ever-after had never felt so perfect. Piper might never stop smiling. And that was fine with her.

* * * * *

Dear Reader,

Wow! I can't believe we are at the end of the Raven Pass books. I have had so much fun with this made-up town, and have especially enjoyed getting to help people "visit" Alaska, my favorite state, through these stories. If you ever make it up here, there is no real town of Raven Pass to visit, but the views along Turnagain Arm are real, and the real-life town of Girdwood is similar to Raven Pass in some ways.

In this book, both Piper and Judah struggle with their view of God. Piper doesn't realize how much God values her and cares about her, and Judah doesn't understand how involved God is in his daily life. Wherever you are in your walk with God right now, if I could tell you anything, it would be that He loves you. At its core, that was the lesson both characters had to learn, and it's one I need to learn over and over again, as well.

I love hearing from readers! I don't know if you know how often God uses you to encourage me, but it seems like every time I really need some help to keep working hard, God has a reader send me a note. Thank you for all your sweet words over the years. If you'd like to send me a note, you can reach me at sarahvarland@gmail.com or find me online at Facebook.com/sarahvarlandauthor.

Sarah Varland

LOVE INSPIRED

INSPIRATIONAL ROMANCE

UPLIFTING STORIES OF FAITH, FORGIVENESS AND HOPE.

Join our social communities to connect with other readers who share your love!

Sign up for the Love Inspired newsletter at **LoveInspired.com** to be the first to find out about upcoming titles, special promotions and exclusive content.

CONNECT WITH US AT:

f Facebook.com/LoveInspiredBooks

🐦 Twitter.com/LoveInspiredBks

Facebook.com/groups/HarlequinConnection